I0698869

ANA'S ODYSSEY

Copyright © 2025 by Mariana Gumm

All rights reserved. This book or any portion thereof may not be reproduced or used in any manner whatsoever without the express written permission of the publisher except for the use of brief quotation in a book review.

ISBN: 978-1-969865-66-4 Paperback
ISBN: 978-1-969865-67-1 Ebook

Rev. date: 12/09/2025

ANA'S ODYSSEY

The Beginning

Mariana Gumm

THE BEGINNING

"I don't live in the past,
I use it to push me forward to the future" Ana

When we come to the world, we come because it occurred to someone, by twist of fate, or simply by accident. Thus, a small and innocent human being is born, and at the expense of who brought it to the world. Totally vulnerable and helpless, stretching her arms as if she would like to hold on to something or someone for her survival. Her small brain is like a blank notebook, her memory assimilates and builds up everything that occur in her environment.

Completely dependent on her mother by instinct and her father out of necessity, the new born starts to watch and accommodates what is given and what its needed to survive. Her emotional development starts from the first moment of her creation. The circumstances of its origin would mark its beginning on the road of life. The feelings transmitted at the precise moment in which the new being is conceived–though parents don't even imagine it–will determine her perception of life.

So far there are few statistics on the topic of conception. Few dare to speak of the purpose of human life or of the role of a new being might have in this world. There are many parents who think that childbearing is the solution to their own needs of affection, acceptance, or affection they did not receive by their predecessors. Therefore they focus on thinking that the new being they engender will compensate them of what is missing in their life. That the new born will become an investment to fulfill their needs. What the newly born compensate them will mark her future for good or for bad.

The human being is born with instinct of survival as any other living being. The genetic heritage of her parents and her intelligence determine much of its character. Her life strategy is based on a way that she can satisfy her primary needs. Is there where begins the struggle between the ego and the superego, be oneself or pretending to please and be accepted "the survival of the fittest". The baby begins to observe what is likable to others and what dislike them also. So she chooses what most suits her either be complacent and obedient or accept the consequences of being her authentic self.

When she claims her uniqueness or pretend to escape the reality that she has to live leads to many uncertainties. And thus begins the game of trial and error. Her reality then begins to be dictated by everything that surrounds her through the years to come. The little one have her fantasy of what she would like to be, but brothers, fellow playmates, classmates of school, teachers, family, and religion dictate her new image. If the new image is acceptable, positive, strong and safe the child is lucky and has a brilliant future. But as in the majority of cases not so, the result could be weakness, negativity, insecurity and rejection then self-esteem is affected and therefore personal values also change. And as a result the unique, original and authentic being has been consumed by others. This is where the conflict is generated and determines the success or failure of the aspirations of that new life.

INHIBITION AND DOUBT

During the second year of life the infant begins to discover that there is something more to her crib and her mother with whom she has remained all this time. She discovers that there are other people trying to communicate with her (him). Then she carefully observes their facial expressions and tone of their voices, is the time to discover how she may be related to the environment that surrounds her. Suddenly she realizes that she is not alone and that there is someone else than her mother and her father, then she sees facial expressions and her mind begins to expand. Now she will have to learn to imitate what works and what is counterproductive. To see the acceptance of others and to choose which is more functional and mixed it with her own repertoire. It begins the exploration of being accepted or rejected. And depending on this, her brain registers those actions that will give her a compensation and those that may cause her problems. Then it comes shame and doubt that eventually become the foundation of her self-esteem.

When the baby begins to take its first steps her brain also changes. It is the age of exploring the outside world. So is the case of the little Ana who is trying to explore her environment. She tries to get out of the chair in which her mother keeps her tied up so "it does not fall." She finally manages to break out and tries to get on another chair. Her frustrated mother speaks out "Ana get off that chair!" then the little one thinks that it is a challenge and do it again, "! Ana! What's wrong with you? Get in that chair." Then her mother intensifies the tone of voice, her face turns red, her lips are tight, her neck is taut, and then takes Ana by her arm as if it were a rag doll, "If you do it again, you will be sorry" by that time the infant does not understand why her mother is so angry and threatening, for Ana that attempt is just a game but seems to be a big mistake. For Ana is a challenge, something to test her own persistence.

The fact that she could fall and hurt herself, is not recorded in her small brain. What her mind registers is that her mother is very angry and her brain records a message "my MOM does not like me." And her world begins to fall apart, her self-worth needs have been broken. All what little Ana wants is to be loved and accepted as it is. Her mind does not assimilate that her mother may be tired or frustrated with the other activities of her daily living. The mind of Ana begins to wonder what have she done that is making her mother so angry? And the doubt appears, what is wrong? Rather than listening to some explanation, everything she sees is anger and rejection. There is nothing of what she expected, affection and patience to teach what it is right or wrong. Everything Ana listens are scolding words. Thus doubt and shame (guilt) start to grow, then she believes that she is not a good person.

Ana has begun the path of low self-esteem. A spot has appeared in the mirror which before was clean and reflected a clear image, now its image is distorted. Henceforth this little incident that for others is insignificant, for the little Ana means the acceptance or rejection of herself. The seed of doubt has begun to germinate, and remains in her mind affecting her future decisions and intelligence, as well as her failures or her triumphs to come.

IGNORANCE AND POVERTY

Ignorance and poverty seeders of misery and other calamities. They are present in the majority of the fatalities. They are also the root of many diseases, both physical and mental and consequently erupt in social problems. In many cultures, it is considered that the fact of being born female makes you less important than any other human being. The first sign of ignorance is shown in the belief that "surname" can only continue in their "sons." Since women "lose" the surname taking the surname of their husband. Besides that they also brake continuity of the dynasty of the "Man of the House." They have the bright idea that the surname makes the person, it would be very interesting to hear the response of that kind of people when someone ask them what is the last name of God or Jesus's last name. Perhaps no one had noticed that is never mentioned in any book of the Holy Scripture?

The second idea of the selfish man is that he wants the male child to resemble him. Without even suspecting that according to the theory of genetics, there is a 75% chance that the child will look more after his mother. While the female child inherits the genetics of her father. Regardless of their origin, the name is just that a "surname", while Genetics is as strong as the color of blood. So when the selfish man (or narcissistic) comes to see himself in his sons, what he is really seeing is the image of his wife reflected in their beloved children. While relegated of his love and acceptance the daughter is really who inherit its character and in many cases his physical features.

The third idea about women is that they generate more expenses than revenues (another big myth). The narcissistic man always hopes to have its image reborn in a "male." Since apparently the men "produce profits" and spend less than the woman. Commonly, when the woman gives birth to a child, the first concern of the man is if it was a girl or a boy instead of asking if the mother is OK. If is a girl, the first expression is: "other expense!" or "more money thrown in the trash." As if the newborn had an opinion to be procreated or begotten. Then it comes to their mind the cost of the new life could be even worse if she was born sickly. And they think: how much money will cost until it is capable of producing any profit? "Sacrifice!" is it worth the effort? But they don't think that were the adults who without thinking of a third; joined their poor needs of self-preservation. Has ever occur to anyone that there may be a need to preserve the specie (human), unconditional affection or respect for the new life? Not even dreaming about the idea that children are "product of love." If someone with good judgment mention it, they deem her (him) crazy or as if that person was from another planet. And they even ask if the person ate something that made her (him) "lose its mind."

THE PROPHECY HAS COME TRUE

In this particular case, the problem becomes more evident when the little Ana is sick for the first time; the father comment would come out as I said "pure waste." As if no baby would became sick as part of their normal development. The little Ana had fallen ill and the fear of "spend time or money" was more than the fear of knowing that the disease could complicate. But thanks to home remedies for stomach pain, it passed soon. So far it was only diarrhea, and force of survival of the baby help it to recover soon. It was discovered afterwards that the baby had drank milk that was spoiling. There was no fresh milk for the girl and asking for milk to neighbors or borrow from the compadres was "embarrassing." As a result, Ana would have to conform only with the "rice milk". Rice carbohydrates that would keep her alive for a good time. Life will continue as nothing important had happened.

Shortly after, the 'Lady of the House" gave the good news to her "loving husband", she was pregnant once again! That gave the man an immense joy, now life gave them another chance to recover from the error of having fathered a baby girl. Now they were careful in the process of the making and "God" would give them a "machito" (a boy). No one then thought that babies need food, clothes, attentions, and time. It was then that they used the most common sayings "where eats one, two, eat" and it was probably true, but parents had to provide them healthy and nutritious food to the two. But would it be enough? If they had not enough for the first child of the family, as it was expected how would they have enough to provide for the second? But there was no complaint because "God could punish them!"- As if the act of giving birth to children for personal satisfaction was an act commanded by God-. So instead of complaining about it, they had to proliferate hoping that family situation would get improved.

Life gave Ana's parents a new opportunity. This time will be a smart, healthy and strong boy, -those were their wishes-. The months went by, and the blissful awaited day arrived. The creature was born, and as they dreamed it was "blonde" and this time was male. What joy a dream come true! Now the attention was for the newborn. And apparently he was well. But as all babies, a few days later he became ill. His mother tried to cure him the same way that Ana had healed with home remedies. But the bottles of Chamomile tea and other remedies were not effective. And the comments started, " he must need some Sun tan" people said, poor "güero" was so weak that it looked like gelatin and as white as snow. After trying with all kind of home remedies, they would look for other alternatives. This time they would see the doctor.

Ana's parents gathered some money and undertook the journey to visit the doctor. They returned home with some medicines and the doctor suggested them to return in a few days. However, it seemed that the "guero" situation worsened, his parents decided to seek a second opinion. To find out after the second opinion, that there was not much to do. The problem was fairly advanced and the doctor told them it was not much hope for life, and probably there was nothing else to do to save the "guero". With disappointment and sadness in their minds they returned to the ranch, thinking its "guerito" would not survive. But as it was so beautiful,–the blondie boy-, it was difficult to accept the loss and the opinion of the doctors. So the parents decided to look for alternative medicine. The prophecy was fulfilled, but conversely, guero was "more expensive" to maintain than the little Ana...

Some people had informed Ana's parents about a "miracle healer" who had saved others from death. This healer lived in the recesses of the Sierra Madre that divided the two States of Nuevo Leon and Tamaulipas, Mex. So again hope shone to "guero". The parents saddled the Mules and prepared some "fittings" and of course stripped Ana out of her blanket of beads and pink squares to cover the "guero", since she didn't need it so much as the sick one according to their parents. Ana would stay with Grandma for a change.

Several days went by, and finally "the miracle healer" gave hope of life to the guerito. To complete the picture they also pay a visit to the "Virgin of Trickle." To thank her for the salvation of the guero. After prayer and everything else, guero's parents were a little more relaxed.

But just in case, they got the "brilliant idea" that if guero died, they should seek "the replacement." And they put themselves in action. No matter that the mother was quite weak, anemic and exhausted. And as nature was thus spawned the spare. Days later they arrived back home. With the revived guero, their bodies reflecting the fatigue of the journey and the malnourished Lady exhausted and "very pregnant." No one was thinking on the complications of the situation, not only the Lady could lose the "spare", but it also could endanger her life. Soon they forgot the recommendation of the healer that they should take a very good care of "guero", since they had rescued him from the clutches of death.

THE FAMILY CONTINUED GROWING

A few months later a baby "the replacement" was born. Although guero survived his illness, the poor baby boy was so "enclenque" (frail) that he could not even walk when the following son was born. The replacement came out brown "morenito" as his father, but nobody said anything since it was at least a "machito". As his father dreams. Because it cost much work to take care of two babies in diapers, they had to use the following online to help babysit. Ana was there, and since she was very independent, they had to train her to take care of the brothers. The baby boys were tied together both from their respective seats, mother giving them their bottles and Ana had to take care of them. Ana would hardly have 5 years when she had to be the nanny of her two brothers. For her, it was fun to see how the younger finished first and took the bottle from guero to finish it. So it was then when her brothers became its entertainment and she forgot that she had to play with other children.

Life had become a routine for Ana's mother, after the other troubles only what was left was to continue with the tradition followed by others. There was no one who would think about another way of life. And as most were poor and ignorant, they only had to continue with the routine, but nobody would attempt to change the situation or it would be a betrayal to the tradition of the others. The game had to go on... So between moans and complaints of poverty and desolation, life continued. Between discussions and more, Ana's parents continued their career of proliferation. As it was always the same story, Mrs. Igna had already resigned to that destiny, and don Ira only cared to prove that he could be as "macho" as the rest of the ranchers and that he would be stronger and more important particularly if his wife had many sons. It would not mattered that the children were full of lice and parasites as well as sickly and malnourished, since all the kids from the ranch were like that and eventually they will "get better."

Months later she (Igna) was again pregnant. Waiting to deliver another "machito". Although the Lady said that she remained always hoping that this time her dream would come true of having a girl with curly/ blond hair with green or blue eyes, and as white as snow. The truth was that what came out were all boys. And as said, in a few months the next baby was born. This time came out blond and pale, and to the delight of Don Ira it was a boy! When people came to visit the Lady, they did not stop saying, "how beautiful, it looks like a Cherub." They doubted he was son of Don Ira since he was brawn morenito. They did not know that there was possibility of offspring of white people in the two families. By the side of Don Ira, he was the only "brown" his deceased siblings were white as well as his sisters according to rumors from those who knew them. And by Mrs. Igna her father was a descendant of white Spaniards who were mostly Caucasian.

With the arrival of the newest member of the family, the other children who already did not fit in the bed of wires, had to sleep on the cold floor, with rags of leftovers of the blankets from their parents. And while they slept in a decent bed of thick mattresses. Ana slept on the floor in pieces of blankets. And of course the Cherub who cried all night and bounced the crib against the wall completed the picture of the happy family. In the morning, the Lady would still sleepy and tired like everyone else, because the Cherub was quite uneasy. The Lady had to light a fire to cook breakfast. With great sacrifice could Mrs. Igna set the fire, because sometimes even oil was not enough, or wood chips to initiate the fire were scarce! But she was trying with bits of paper and some wood chips (cascaras) that Ana had collected the previous day. After a cloud of smoke, and a few tears, the fire had erupted. Ana didn't know if those tears were caused by smoke or by their sad fate. It would be another ordeal now to know if there would be enough sugar to sweeten the tea, not even thinking about a glass of milk. Since only asking for it sounded like an insult. So only the "Man of the House" had the right to drink some milk if it was some, and the children would have to accept a spout "pintadita" of milk in the tea. No need to mention the lunch and dinner.

In the winter the situation was even worst, since the water froze, and formed a layer of ice on the cooked corn, which Ana was responsible for washing to get it ready to grind and preparing the dough for tortillas. The small hands of Ana would bend and hurt and her fingers twisted with the cold ice but she had to earn her breakfast. Then she had to help grind the corn as well to produce the tortillas which would feed the family for the rest of the day. The entire process would take the whole morning. Then she had to help to care for the children, and in the evening to bring water from the well or the creek to cook and take care of the other need, since there was not running water in the whole ranch. Ana's hands were a true disaster, dry and cracked by the cold, the only thing that could cure them was lard which reduced dryness and prevented the bleeding. Even lotion or cream for hands was not affordable.

NATURE AND PARENTING

Some psychologists and experts who work in the science of human behavior, claim that people relate to and identify with those who have complimented the needs of affection, such as emotional support, love, and acceptance. In Ana's life, there were not many people with whom she could identify or serve as example of life (role model). The few could be counted on the fingers of one hand and there were some fingers left. Among them was the maternal grandfather, the aunt Lolita, Nana, and first elementary school teachers. Others were unknown people approaching her for good or bad to "test" the reaction of Ana, as transient traders who pass by selling trinkets and the photographers who gave her a treat if she sang a song to them or dance something, also occasionally they took a photograph which her mother made disappeared later since it was not to her delight.

Ana's maternal grandfather had awakened her imagination with anecdotes and stories. Grandpa's favorite phrase was "one who has it, is because it has cost him and deserves it." And some tales of treasures. The grandfather used to say that people who have money is because they work hard and know how to use the resources properly. He usually got up at 4:00 A.M in the morning, ate some breakfast and packed some supplies in his backpack and started working at the milpa (field) if it was good season for sowing. If not he would go to his huerta (orchard) to irrigate and fertilize the fruit trees. Although he had people who worked for him, he was the first arriving and the last to leave the site. The journeys were 12 to 14 hours a day. Apart from the cornfields, grandfather had cows, goats, and swarms of honey for each season of the year.

Grandpa never went to school but had much common sense and knew that loving what someone does for living, enriches not only the spirit, but also the "Pocket". Its vast variety of trees was the most comprehensive of the ranch including a wide variety of apples trees, peaches, oranges, pomegranates, avocados, and prickly pears. At home no one would miss the Wattles hanging from the formwork with at least a dozen cheeses, pots with barrel-shaped of honey classified by season and type of flower. Also fruit preserves and "gorditas" from oven. It was a real delight for Ana to go and visit grandpa's home since it was like another world far different from her home.

The grandfather was respected by his reputation as a "Maker of Fortune" thanks to his talent, his best investment was to buy gold and silver. It was also the lender of the ranch. Although he never went to school he was able to calculate percentages by memory and knew how much his debtors owed him. People commented that the grandfather buried jars and bags of gold and silver and that nobody knew where or how he did it.

Among the favorite tales that grandfather narrated was the "treasure of the cave". In a place away from the path of passers-by there was a cave in which strings and chains sounds were heard at midnight and also a voice was heard saying: *"all or nothing."* One day a pedestrian heard the noise and voice, but as he was afraid of it, decided to tell his best friend and compadre. He entrusted him his suspicion that there could be gold in that place. But the compadre's ambition aroused and he was convinced at first that both would explore the place when night would be enough obscure in the next new moon. However knowing where the cave was, the compadre's temptation was bigger than friendship. So one night before the designated date, the second decided to do it alone without help from the first. When he went to the cave, he waited for it was sufficiently obscure. Just at 12:00 midnight, he heard the sound of chains and the voice saying *"or all or nothing"* the compadre said I want *"all"*.

Then the voice guided him to what he wanted. As his wish the pots appeared in front of his eyes, but they were sealed and heavy. He carried them to a safe place and when he could open them, he realized that someone had played him a joke. Instead of gold and silver coins, the pots were full of mud and excrement. He then decided to go to the compadre's house and damp them over. The house of the compadre had a gate on the roof, with a big effort he climbed onto the roof, opened the gate of the ceiling and damped all the big pots on the compadres' bed, saying *"there it goes and enjoy it."* The following morning the compadre found the nice surprise, then he went and look for the second and told him with a mocking smile, "And how you woke up this morning?" the first said to the second, "a miracle has occur." "Someone left me a gift on my feet, a lot of gold and silver coins, I think someone went ahead to see our "cave" and it didn't like what he saw! And here is a proof to what I telling you, and gave him some coins this is for "being the best friend of the world." The PostScript of the tale was that morbid ambition always ends badly and that if "someone have it is because he deserves it".

Grandpa always told many stories and Fables, apart from the treasures, also said that the women were so good to give birth, that instead of giving birth "they lay little babies" as the hens. And he was telling stories that almost nobody would remember by the time he returned to his house, but nobody imagined that they had been engraved in Ana's memory, as messages for the future.

The next person on the list of people who left an imprint on Ana's mind was the aunt Lolita. She was the widow of Ana's uncle. Lolita was the healer, clerk, and artisan who made clay griddles to make a living. She had 3 children, Tota, Nana and Mago. Whenever Ana suffered from any type of affliction, she ran to Lolita's house and asked her to make her a remedy. Depending on the symptoms, of the illness Lolita would prepare a remedy for Ana. Either "mal de ojo" ear or flu infection, and the bad vibes etc. For the "mal de ojo", she would use an egg passing it through all Ana's body and praying many sentences of spirits, after finishing the ritual, Lolita emptied the egg into a glass of water to make the bad sprit go away or dissolve in the water. Whether it was effective remedy or not for what it was worth it made Ana feel relieved... For the "espanto", Lolita swapped Ana with a broom of ash bush (wild lavender) all over her body with prayers of recovery of the spirit, -spirit of Ana don't delay or get lost- Ana had to answer – here I go-. For some rare reason, Lolita rationalized the illnesses of Ana, and said that it was because Ana was very perceptive of her environment and since most of people who surrounded her had negative energy that would make Ana sick. Maybe there was a part of truth on Lolita's theory, because when Ana grew up she was able to perceive people's vibes and energy faster than the rest of people she knew.

For the "bad vibes" Lolita used "the stone of fire" which was a -crystal like- stone that she thought had a "healing powers." After passing it all over Ana's body and praying, she burned it in the fire of the chimney and before Ana's eyes there was the "bad thing," it was probably Ana's childish imagination, but she could find a different shapes after the stone transformed with the heat of the fire. For protection Lolita would give her a necklace with a brown ball called "ojo de venado" or "tiger eye" and said that it would absorb the "bad vibes", but since Ana was very sensitive to all type of energy, she constantly attracted very strong vibes which would break the amulet, when Ana realized it the necklace had fulfilled its task, but due to the force of it, it broke the amulet in a half and Ana ran again to Lolita's home to look for another. Apart from caring for Ana's spiritual illnesses Lolita also took care of Ana's hair. Sometimes Ana would go for days with her dirty and unkempt long hair. Ana's mother had no time to comb it and therefore only Lolita had the patience to do it since she had too much hair and very long which was a real hassle for Ana's mother.

Nana was the eldest daughter of Lolita, she had grown up and someone had taken her working as a maid in the city. When she came back to the ranch she brought gifts for her family and did not forget about Ana. In fact since nobody gave anything to Ana, Nana wanted to give her the first doll which unfortunately, she did not enjoy for long. Ana watched with curiosity that box with a blue-painted happy face doll with her hair in the shape of bun. Ana's mother had kept it from her so "she would not destroy it" and therefore Ana could only watch it from afar on the highest shelf.

After several months, Nana was visiting and asked Ana if she still had the doll she gave her as a gift. Ana had no idea that the box with the cute doll was for her. It was then that Nana graved the box with painted doll and gave the doll to Ana. Then Nana asked her mother why she had not gave Ana the doll before. Ana's mother replied that she did not want Ana to destroy it. That day Nana and Ana played a long time with the doll and it was so much joy that Ana slept hugging the doll embracing it as if it were the most precious treasure. The next day Ana's mother asked her to return it. And she put it back and kept it in the blue box. Whenever Ana wanted to play with the doll, her mother would gave to her only if she had time to monitoring it so Ana would not break it.

After a while Ana's mother invented excuses to not give her the doll. Ana gave up and did not insist on asking her for the doll anymore. On one occasion Ana was looking for something that had fallen under the bed where her mother and father slept. It was then she discovered the doll's head! With her face full of surprise and sadness Ana ran to show her mother the doll's head. Her mother then said "what did I tell you, everything you touch you destroy, there was a reason why I didn't gave it to you before" Ana could not understand her mother comment and walked away with doubt in her face. How could she forget or did not remember how she dismembered the doll she liked so much, and how could she do it? The most bizarre thing was that the doll's body was never found.

After that Ana learned to make her own toys, with the stems of the pumpkin' leaves she made flutes, with slats of wood "rumbadores," and with bags of paper and plastic made balls. After all Ana had no longer time to play, as she had to take care of her siblings who had become the dolls she never had. And thus, little 5 year old Ana became the nanny, the cook, the maid which helped with the cleaning and the milling, brought water from the stream or well and dish washer, and washing machine for the diapers of her brothers. And if she made a complaint or resistance she would face the consequences.

THE RESIGNATION

Ana's mother (Dona Igna) had her own–very peculiar- way of thinking, after accepting that her fate was already marked by her decision taken long time ago–when trying to follow a dream, left her family where nothing was missing-, Mrs. Igna finally realized that she had to resign herself (accept her destiny) and "endure the rod" as said by her husband Don Ira. Now she had a husband to whom she had to obey, with "duties" and "responsibilities." With just 30 years of age and "a bunch" of kids there was no other option, nor was any way out (to escape) from that destiny.

Either way, there were not many choices to reach out; after all no one would offered an alternative since all or most of the people thought alike due to the lack of resources and education. The ladies -who had not passed third grade- or some that could not even write their name, as a result, they did not know any other way to survive. Igna saw no other output of that commitment that had been cast in tow. And she accepted her fate and follow "the orders" and met the demands of the "law". Don Ira, her husband was the "law", who apart from thinking that he was always right, his voice was the authority, and no one could discuss any of his ideas, no matter if they were so out of reality. And if someone in the family dared to challenge them, the situation would worsen.

To not complicate matters further and to continue a life of survival, Mrs. Igna took as her "daily bread" Don Ira's orders. Thus, her main duty would be or was to give him as many sons as possible, no matter the living conditions in which they lived. But Igna had an "only dream" a blonde blue eyed and white skin girl. As she would said that God did not give her that wish, but at least she had sons "gueritos" which diminished her feelings of guilt. As Igna had no confidence to express her thoughts to others, Ana was her "handkerchief for tears." She probably believed that being (little) "Chiquita" Ana wouldn't remember or understand a thing. What Inga didn't know was that Ana had a memory as good as an "elephant." Although some of the confessions of Igna were mean and hurt Ana's dignity, particularly the idea of Mrs. Igna "having a blonde girl with colored eyes". For Ana, it meant that she was not worthy of the affection and acceptance of her mother.

Ana's efforts to win the affection of her mother had not been sufficient which for Ana represented a big challenge to earn a bit of affection to feed her soul and spirit. Due to poverty and deprivation, a bit of affection would be the only thing that did not cost money that was Ana's thought. Later on, Ana would discover that poor Igna was not able to emanate that maternal love or affection for one simple reason, the mother of Inga had died when she was young (a toddler), and as a result her mind and heart had frozen (disconnected from feelings) and as it was difficult to turn on the fire every day, so was difficult to light the fire of the maternal love, particularly when Ana was far from being "the girl of her dreams."

INCLINATIONS TOWARDS POLITICS

They were the beginnings of the 1970s, time of elections for Governor and President of the Republic. It was customary that the candidates did campaign to collect votes, although everyone knew that the party in "power" would win anyway, the candidate of the party in power had won for generations. But the most important thing was that when he walked in campaign the crew gave away "food". Everything began with the gubernatorial candidate who gave "milk powder" for all malnourished children of the ranch. It was like a "beacon of light for hope" that things would improve in the future. Lots of packages of powdered milk were distributed according to the size of the family. So the family of Ana had a good chance of collecting a large portion of milk powder. Don Ira had confirmed his theory that "there is no evil that good doesn't overcome." And although he could not complain of what it had wanted to (be careful what you wish for), because he fathered many sons, the reality was felt like the wind in his face.

There were times of campaign and changes, people gathered at the local school to make a feast to welcome the candidates. Then the people wore their best outfits. They also bathed and combed their hair to look at their best appearance. Ana was six years old, but as her mom needed her to help with the chores they had not registered her yet in school. So she had to be creative and make arrangements to go to school as "a listener" without even being officially enrolled as student. She would hide in the back of the classroom so no one would notice her presence, except sometimes the teacher would wonder what that girl was doing in there.

It was customary to prepare a student from the class to read the "welcoming speech". The teacher would then choose a student who was good to speak in public and was not shy or timid to speak in front of important people as the candidate for Governor of the State was... For

Ana, that was not big problem. What was a problem was that she did not know well how to read or write either, and she was not even officially registered as student of the class. What she had was good memory and willingness to help. When the time came to welcome the Governor, the teacher had chosen the student who read better to welcome him. As Ana knew that she didn't have many possibilities of public speaking, she had memorized the speech that had been given to the smart student that would read it to the candidate. But just in case, Ana had asked parents to buy her a decent dress even second hand used and shoes since she only had worn sandals. The idea she had created in her mind was that if the chosen "smart student" was not performing right, she would "jump to the rescue."

And the much anticipated day arrived, the template was ready and adorned. The Act was ready, people were gathered and expecting the arrival of the candidate to welcome him, lined up in a row behind the curtains were the children who will present the speech, and so was Ana (hidden)wearing her only "decent" dress that her parents could get her. Ready the audience and everything seemed in harmony. Ana with her memorized speech was placed behind the bandstand to wait for her time. When the chosen student started to stutter, Ana came to the rescue. With great pride arose as student of the school, but with the overwhelming emotion the original speech was forgotten. But she decided then to improvise, "Welcome Mr. candidate to this Ranch poor, "arrabalero", unpaved and full of muleteers, donkeys with much pride." The embarrassed teacher stopped the speech and withdrew Ana from the stage. But the candidate smiled and thought that she was very funny and to validate her courage and effort gave her several notebooks and pencils. To Ana that was more than enough, for she never had a decent notebook, so those notebooks and pencils were like the lottery prize. Now, there would be no excuse for not going to school. Although her parents had other plans for her.

ANA'S PREDESTINATION.

"You do not prepare the path for the children, just prepare them for the path" (Popular saying)

Ana's parents had thought that they would use her to "assist" Igna since Ana did not complain about the work (house chores). The idea was that being female, could only serve to be housewife (if she would get to that point) and school was as a "waste of time", and therefore Ana did not need to go to school, because "she had better things to do at home." But Ana had not resigned to the fate that her parents had traced for her. Such as caring for her siblings, help with cleaning and other chores. Conversely, Ana escaped when she could to go to school. She would take her notebook and pencil and her small chair (or banquito) and sat in the back of the classroom so would not disrupt the class. At the end of class was the first who would run quickly to avoid being "regañada" (scolded). Although at home, she would not avoid the consequences of her actions; as she had left the children without care and they needed her for "something", of course they had already noticed her absence and therefore she deserved a punishment. Don Ira was waiting for her with his belt in his hand to give her "what she deserved" and if she escaped the next day the marks of the belt would cause her shame when children would see her legs marked by the "cintarazos" that sometimes would break her skin and stay for a long time.

But for Ana no human force or punishments would stopped her, one day the teacher felt sorry for her, and rather than punish her, decided to talk to her parents to enroll her formally in the class. Ana was fearful of her parents could thought that she was causing problems at school. So when the teacher arrived to her home, she hid behind the door to listen to the conversation. After a long conversation, the teacher had convinced her parents that would do her well to know how to read and write properly, and that she had "the right" to learn to read as the rest of the children. As on other occasions Ana had explained her parents that she would like to learn "something in life", since what she saw to her surroundings was not "pleasant at all". And that apart she would not be as "rude" as the others. In her mind the idea that teachers know how to change the mentality of others had been created, and therefore they could also help to change her life. Only then her parents finally accepted that Ana really wanted to go to school, but that would not help her to avoid to do chores, she would have to manage her time between school and home tasks since that was the only way "things were" at that time.

THE YEARS 70S AND ITS CHANGES

It was the time of the elections for President of the Mexican Republic. And the custom was that the candidates for President would visit the most recondite points of the country, although was not new to do so knowing that the majority of the population was poor and ignorant, and therefore was not difficult to convince them to vote in his favor. The ranch was partying again. The poor farmers (peasants) had been influenced by the ruling party and to cooperate had to paint propaganda with painting of three color official party, green, white and red. Thus during the evening the poor farmers painted large ads in the hills and walls of what was called a "road".

The signs said "above the peasants, down the chiefs, vote for the PRI." Ana was observing cautiously the effort of people in working to make the giant signs. Then she asked, "What does vote mean...? No one could give a logical explanation. And only showed her ballots that had a circle of different colors. Just by across a circle they would elect the President. But how they knew if it was best for the country? The responses were the same "because it is the party of the poor." And the adults told Ana do not ask more questions and to wait to 'grow up' so she could understand well things. Signs that the peasants painted lasted not much in the night the offended "chiefs" would destroyed them, and again the following week farmers painted them again. Ana thought then than it does not matter how old the people grow, they always fought as children do.

Time went by and days later, Ana saw a few trucks coming full of gifts, particularly "cookies". The PRI party candidate had won the presidency. And as a first gift he was sending greetings to the poor: *cookies*. Again, that reinforced the idea that "better times will always come" as Don Ira said. Then many children in the family benefited from the president's charity, since the more kids they had in a family, the more boxes of cookies they could collect. With so many kids at home as Ana's family had, they could eat as much cookies they eat to fill them up and even they suffered from indigestion. Family didn't eat anything else for several days until the cookies were gone.

Everyone had voted for the PRI, even children (and a few cadavers of dead people) who had no age to vote. The promises of "abundance and better times" to come had stimulated the only thing they were used to do in the ranch "making more babies." Even the elected President sent a photograph to all families with his beautiful family of 10 children with their respective offspring and wives. That left no doubt that if the President set the example of reproduction of children desperately, then it was a very good example to follow. Consequently, why not to imitate the "good example" and continue what most people had already begun would be a foolish idea. The idea had been reinforced, having children was "the best way to leave a mark on this world" and show their legacy.

The logic or common sense did not exist then at the ranch. The President came from a dynasty of highly educated people and not only political but economical high class too. So they could have all the children that their nature allowed them, since they had sufficient resources to feed them and educate them. This was not the case of ignorant peasants and with little or nothing to offer to their malnourished and sickly children, or their malnourished and tired wives. Lands were becoming sterile, and the rains did not fell so consistently (there was a drought!), therefore nothing served so much politics when reality was still hitting the innocent people, particularly to powerless children.

OVERPOPULATION AND PROLIFERATION

The era of the 70s promised hope and "prosperity" since the new President with his "beautiful family" had convinced the population- mostly the poor- that they could also do the same as him or follow his example. As a result, nobody would think in another "thing" but the reproduction–no one could be happier -. As told by the men that if the President set the example being who he was, then those who did not have money "nothing to lose" with much reason could continue the reproduction. And everyone was on task. If they had a child at least every two years, now they would have one a year, and also twins. There was no much difference in Ana's home, there was nothing to debate or argue. Specially, when they have nothing to lose, but "work until you drop" as Don Ira said, "don't be a coward".

Ana's parents, were not married by the Church due to the "rush" since they thought that it was better to proliferate soon instead, and save for the future. But how much could have cost a wedding if love was worth it? But in this case it was more the need of having a woman in the house and see their offspring multiply, than to see if that could give them a bit of happiness. The opportunity knock the door to make the marriage blessed… As part of the changes –for better life- the Government had implemented a campaign of "evangelization" since people would multiply also they had to do it as "God commanded" under the blessing of the Church.

To make it all more formal, several couples would receive the blessing in group. As most of them already had a lot of children, they were not allowed to dress in white, only had to use a decent dress. Mrs. Igna designed a dress grey blue which was her favorite color. To Ana that was the saddest color her mother could choose since it reflected only that, sadness. But so what, who would care about the opinion of a seven years old girl? So all gathered in one of the houses that the father (priest) had chosen. The father gave them the "blessing" and send them home. After the ceremony everyone returned home with the hope that if they were now "blessed" everything would be easier and they could overcome all the "adversity." With six kids and a life full of troubles and poverty, Mrs. Igna and Don Ira believed that the fact of being married by the Church would improve their quality of life by art of "Faith."

Reality always beat them, as the winter wind hits the bare face. The smallest of children, rebel as an "angry cat", used to hit his wooden crib against the wall with such force that sometimes it would hook on the wall and the boy would rolled to the ground. After crying for a good time sitting on the threshold of the door he sat there waiting to be rescued. When the child was angry he would threw a big tantrum and sometimes he would be crawling and crashing his head against the wall, and if this was far, he would drop his head on the ground and then cried like a "kid slaughtered", giving all the commotion, the whole people in the vicinity asked what was going on, and why he was angry and ask his parents "what are you doing with that poor child?".

Mrs. Igna continued the routine and Ana her chores since it took at least half a day to make the tortillas for the whole family. While Ana had to assume the responsibility of caring for the small child, but she did not know how to control him since he was too difficult for a 7-year-old girl. But for Igna that would serve her so she later will be "trained" to be "housewife" because most likely that was her destiny,–if someone "would do her a favor" since the pobrecilla (poor thing) had "nothing to offer" thus, she probably had to learn how to "deserve a man."- Ana had to check if the child had soiled the diaper and as her hands were so little she had to report to Lady Igna so she would change it and then Ana will have to wash it because there was no money to buy disposable diapers.

The little Tuito, continued with his tantrums and awaking everyone at 4:00 AM in the morning. His way of crying was uncontrollable by the minimal thing, either because he was hungry, it was dirty or because he simply had a "colic". To the residents of the ranch it was not rare to hear him crying to the top of his lungs. Observing the situation and above all to avoid the shame of gossiping, his parents decided that they had to seek a solution to the problem. Since they could not find the reason why the child was so rebellious. Among all the ideas was the idea that the child was probably "maloreado" (lost his soul).

They decided then to find a way to "cure" him. But as the healers of the rancho could not "fix" the angry child, probably the best was to take him to the nearest "Holy Saint", who was "San Francisco of Assisi" and promise him as "an offering." So they had to plan a trip and find a way to gather the "money." This time nobody thought that it was much "sacrifice" because of angry child was worth since was "machito and guerito" (blondie and boy). Then, his parents sold the pigs and the chickens they had to be able to raise money for the trip. Although the rest of the family was left at home to eat what they could "beans with tortilla."

Once collected the money and provisions, the couple were ready to travel with the offspring to go see if the faith that they had could "cure" him, or at least that would calm him down a little. They also hoped that the kid would speak clear since nobody understood him when he tried to speak. After a few days, the happy family returned with the child "partially cured", now he was speaking a few words, which was a relief since he could at least say what or why he was so annoyed when he threw tantrums. Never occurred to them thinking that the kid had inherit the character (genes) of his father since Don Ira never solved anything if it wasn't by physical violence. But only with his children, because–he was never challenge one of his size- as Tuito said, when he could say it.

THE OVERPOPULATION
AND SHORTAGES

The Government had realized –finally- that misleading people by allowing them to reproduce like a "fashion sport" had caused some problems of overpopulation. The demographic explosion had been speed up like a space shadow. The drought had sharpened and food production was significantly reduced. Hunger prevailed in most of the nation. Then noticing the crisis, the Government implemented different programs of "social awareness." The first strategy was to increase the self-esteem of women so they could start to make a better "use of the brain" in a more efficient manner. And so it was born the "International Year of the Woman."

The right of "voice" was now given to "the woman", but men though that women would only waste their time, the movement of "liberation" was not what they thought would be. If the plan of "awakening of that long dream of submissive and obedient woman" worked, then the second part of the plan would be to educate the husbands. But first they (government) had to "wake up" the woman of her "State of Automaton", and the women shall abandon the old role of being obedient, resigned, and do everything that the man demanded; mainly they had to said "no" when needed to stop proliferation. While the media was trying to remove the woman from the "dark", of her world of submission and devotion, through radio programs and songs that described the new roles of men and women. At the same time was working on awareness for man from his role as a provider and to keep the family in a conscious and efficient manner.

Social workers taught classes on how to use contraceptives and distributed brochures of the necessary care to have healthier children. They also taught the poor as "small family lives better." And to complete the picture, how to do gardening and seed some vegetables for the basic food basket. The family as the basis of a good community should be well fed. Everything sounded quite good, with the only problem that the changes would not happen overnight without the resistance of uneducated peasants who were used to demand and do with their body and family everything they wanted.

In a world where only the opinion of ignorant and macho man governed, all those changes sounded like insults to their "manhood." In the "tendajo" (little market) of the ranch the men gathered to exchange their ideas and opinions about "family orientation" and how they felt wounded – in their pride- by so much "insolence" of social workers who dared to tell the "men" "how to direct their lives." Feeling offended by such "daring"; comments of rejection were very common, "those lazy old ladies, who have no other things to do" "who know nothing about life" -They should be taking better care of their families and let others live, added the men.

Meanwhile in Ana's home her family and her parents tried to digest what they heard in the talks of "family-orientation." Don Ira continued having the idea that women "must obey the men." And so Inga would continue producing children until her body would "give up". He also said that if there was time of "shortage and crisis" also would come times of "abundance", and that the people of the world "must suffer to deserve." Then the revolutionary ideas to change the "status quo" was very difficult, since teachers did not understand "the needs of a man."

Mrs. Igna on the other hand, tired of a life of scarcity and calamities, began to contemplate the possibility of a different life. She was trying to convince Don Ira that he had to explore some options. And -why not -spaced a little the reproduction, at least until they had more food and probably more money to buy the basics for living. Even though striving Igna expose her ideas, it didn't impress Don Ira. He continued saying "you complain too much, if anything you need, there are enough beans and tortillas", and there were some but rotten tortillas and beans with weevils. Meanwhile in the mind of the Lady, it was already began to germinate the seeds of curiosity and hope for a different life.

A good day came up that she had to see a doctor for some ailments that did not seem to cease with home remedies. Mrs. Igna had saved a little money secretly from Don Ira for "contingencies." After asking permission from her husband she embarked on the bus to the town. The "comadre" had received instructions on helping the family to cook dinner for the rest of the children who had been left at home. The "comadre" came home prepared a pan of greasy potatoes with beans and left, leaving Ana to take care of serving dinner and washing dishes. Ana with just 8 years old, would be responsible to see that all was well and organize the kitchen and put the rest of children to sleep.

THE PUNISHMENT

The next day in the afternoon the Lady of the House returned, Mrs. Igna showed a face of remorse and guilt. How was the trip? Asked Don Ira, observing the face of disgust and distrust of Don Ira, the Lady lowered her head and said "well, so." Why what happened? Said don Ira, Igna without being able to hide her guilt replied, "I didn't do nothing wrong, just wanted to get contraceptives." She had talked to the doctor regarding the situation of the family and the doctor had suggested that planning the size of the family was the decision of the couple. In the same way they should decide the number of children who they were able to maintain. If they reach an agreement, the doctor had given her some contraceptives "only to try."

Don Ira frowning his forehead with great authority added, "Those stupid doctors don't know anything of the needs of a man." Besides, "who cares for the doctor's opinion if he won't support my kids," don Ira continued his sermon as if he were disciplined a 10-year-old boy. If you continue with that nonsense ideas, "God will punish you denying his will". The Lady didn't say a word with bowed head looking down the floor, as if she was receiving her well-deserved punishment for trying to challenge the will of the "Lord of the House".

Suddenly Don Ira noticed Igna had a cut on her knee. Then he asked, and what happened to your knee? Doña Inga explained with a great regret that she had fell down from the bus due to nerves and it had scraped her knees. Don Ira then reinforced his scolding saying "what did I say", and even "worse things can happen." As a result, nobody mentioned the subject. A few days later, the Lady began to have nausea and mood changes. Ana, with her innocent curiosity asked them what was really happening or if Igna was sick of something. No one gave a good reason, Ana decided to ask the aunt Lolita what was going on.

The aunt Lolita knew everything that was what Ana thought. Thus, Lolita told Ana that sometimes when women are pregnant they have some aches and pains. When Ana heard the word "pregnancy" felt that a hole in the stomach was just made. She also had the hope that things would improve, but with those news, the dreams of a better life had vanished and the hope of a better life was as far as the horizon. Ana with just eight years old, watched sadly the depressing environment and full of coldness, concerned about her malnourished siblings with lice and rotten clothes. While at the sunset the ladies gathered to talk about their sorrows and complains. They said that lice were coming out of the "pinsion" probably referring to the "depression."

EDUCATION AS PART OF THE SOLUTION

"When someone tell you that 'you can't', it's a thought to be the reflection of their own limitations, not yours" Ana

In Ana's mind was wandering the idea that something had to be done to change the situation. One of her ideas was that she had to work hard so others did not complain of her behavior and thus they could leave her alone to follow her dreams of change. So she continued trying to be useful and help as much as possible and to learn all what she could. Besides trying to find out why adults were doing so many things without "common sense." Apart from going to school in the morning, Ana was returning home to help with the chores, -at her young age- because they (her parents) had assigned activities that would take her the rest of the day. Among them were to bring the water from the well for daily use, washing children's diapers, bring wood to start the fire, also washing dishes cleaning the beans, shelling the corn, and the others as required. And because there was no time during the day to do the homework, she had to do it at night at the light of candles or oil lamp.

In the morning she had to get up from the cold ground with sore and painful body and pretend that all was well. On the night before, she had to collect "paistle" to make her own bed. The first thing she had to do early, was to bring the water from the well to wash the Hominy (nixtamal). After finishing those 2 chores she could ensure the breakfast. Because according to "the law" of Don Ira "If one did not work, did not eat." Which was very clear to Ana, then she had to grind the corn to make the tortillas, sweeping the patio, watch over the kids and make the bed of her parents. With so many chores, Ana forgot that she was entitled to play. Dressed in a beggar's clothes with her long hair that sometimes it was full of "bugs", she was worried about only one thing, "it is any way to get out of this misery."

In her small world with lack of affection, and everything one needs to meet basic needs. The question remained, how was it possible that no one cared about anyone else live in those depressing conditions? In her mind would not fade the idea that the only way out of poverty was probably "education." For her there were no dreams close to "Santa Claus", "Wise Men" or the "Wizard of Oz" those only existed in the books teachers provided her because even those were scarce at the Ranch. Ana had no other distraction more than stargazing at night and read books in the light of the candles. When weariness overcame her, she would go to sleep in her assigned corner, which had been allocated like any baby animal. While her parents slept peacefully in their thick mattress bed, sustained by glass bottles, so nobody would go up and play on the bed.

Among other household activities, Ana was also responsible for "making the bed" of course there was no other than the parents' bed. But she also had to pick up the rags -improvised beds-for children who did not deserved a decent bed. Apart she had to pick up the dirty clothes and empty "the piss of the putty" that her parents had the right to use only because it was for exclusive use of them. Others had to go outside to relieve their needs no matter if it was cold and dark in the night. Ana also swept and shook the dust of the table, apart from watering the dirty floor so that it would not be so dusty. And so it remained her journey. Every day apart from be punished if she would become "oppositional" or the marks of the belt would show the rest of people if she had been disobedient. But the willpower never abandoned her and continued going to school no matter what would happened.

THE DISCIPLINE AS PART OF FAMILY TRAINING

As part of the progress of those times, the Government had decided to improve the "roads of the nation" and in the Ranch to make the "Camino real" better. For which it was needed to expand the "Camino real" and turn it into road that would serve the trucks enter and made delivery of the goods. Suddenly came several trucks full of people with orange helmets, men who directed the project organized a "Board at the school" to inform the peasants as how the process would be, they would use "gunpowder plot holes" which would be very loud and cause the curiosity of the people, so all needed to be cautious about getting close to the area.

The next day the big project- work began. From afar anyone could see men screaming and the rumblings of the holes as well as the dust caused by the same. Ana and her siblings watched curious from a distance what was happening. But a good day the curiosity was bigger than their fear, then when dad was away, they –Ana and her brothers- decided to approach a bit to see the holes of gunpowder explosions. It was a true spectacle to see as giant rocks broke in small pieces (desquebrajaban) as if they were sugar… with the entertaining scene they were mesmerized, so they did not realize that don Ira had discovered them, and as if it was a cyclone arrived with its *"angry wolf face"* and belt in hand. Ana and her brothers literally paralyzed.

Without even explaining why, Don Ira pushed and whip them as if they were donkeys to home. Arriving at the house he stuck them and beaten until they "pee and poop their pants" and until he got tired. He then forced them to clean themselves. As the explanation never came, no one knew the reason for the beating. For only small curses and screams it sounded like hail rain came out of Don Ira's mouth. Days later, only marks of the "cintarazos" and the memories of a punishment that no one knew the reason why it happened, had been etched in the memory of the children.

Don Ira did not know or did not want to "over complicate" his life with explanations. He had been born and raised among animals and had formed himself based on scolding and abuse both by his father and other family members. He had not had time to educate himself or go to school, very barely had reached third grade and he thought that was all he needed to survive. Since "the animals" did not understand lessons or explanations (why bother) it was not necessary to "waste time" going to school. For him, it was more important to know how to work the land and care for the animals. His intellect had not given him for more, and therefore had no patience to talk to the children. Only knew to "hit them" (execute them) in the same way he beat the animals with those he worked in the field.

One fine day Ana "gathered some bravery" and I asked her father why he had so much hatred toward the children, accustomed to the scolding and beatings, she hoped that his father at some point could explain the reason for the beatings and the bad mood and she took the risk of asking. The only response she received was, "if you do not 'execute' the children is because you don't care about them ..." Ana's mind did not find any logic on the explanation and in her little mind only appeared a new question, why adult people love others with hatred? Ana also thought that maybe the two books Don Ira had read during his whole life had not served much. Don Ira boasted that "he knew so much" because he had "two books" which titles ware *how one triumphs in life* and *who are you.* He also said that those books had not been written by a "damn." Ana had no more to say, so she did not insist and withdrew herself from the conversation. While walking away she was thinking she had to read more than "two books" to be able to understand that way of thinking.

READ TO GROW

"That one who asks, arrives to Rome" (people said)

Knowing that the only way to find the answer to her questions would be through the knowledge, Ana thought that the answer could be in the books or in asking others; it was then when Ana decided to dedicate herself to read and ask questions, also she would put more attention when she observed the surroundings. So Ana began to read all the books that crossed her hands. Each reading seemed to open the door to a different world that she knew. She liked stories, cartoons and poems, some in verse or prosa. Whenever she memorized a poem or cartoon, Ana was always sharing it so that she would never forget it. Mainly she shared her readings with her parents, although did not caused them much of surprise, since they had their own stories.

Regardless of the opinion of the parents and ignoring their poor education, Ana shared her experiences with books and so she said to them: would you like to hear something new I learned? They did not answer her, but she would insist, well I will tell you anyway, "how fresh is this morning, air enters through the nose, dogs barking, a child cries, and a plump and pretty girl is grinding corn on a stone..." Ana's parents did not enjoy much Ana's grace, "That is the reason why I don't like that you go to school" said Don Ira, "they teach you pure nonsense stupidities."

"Then show me something interesting" said Ana. "You are crazy, can't you see that we have much to do?" said Mr. Ira "Ana stop being annoying and go to see if "the pig laid an egg." Ana replied, "They do not lay eggs" but maybe women do. Grandfather said that women lay babies. Although I don't think so, because I've never seen that they lay eggs. I have only seen women become so inflamed (like a balloon), and suddenly they say that "the crane brought a baby," to what the Lady said, "get out of here, damn girl." Go get yourself busy, wash clothes, bring water from the creek, or sweep the patio. But Ana was tired of working all day and answered back to her parents, "I don't want to be like you, ignorant." I'm going to go to school to study and make a different life, Ana said. To what her parents said "go to see if those 'books' are going to feed you", said her mother. Ana said just 'watch me', I'm sure they may help somehow.

In those days of the mid-1970s, a missionary nun came to the ranch. She tried to educate the peasants through religion so they teach their children to live better in a quieter home. Ana as always with curiosity, went to chat with the nun and came close to her. Ana then ask the missionary why people like to reproduce in their lives constantly without not even have enough resources for their survival. The nun shook her head and said "one day when you grow up you will understand." Ana then replied, "but I want to know now not later," the missionary said, "now you're just a girl, when you grow up you will get married and you will have kids and a husband," to which Ana replied, "no thanks, I will never getting married, or having many children and much less a nag husband..." The nun tried to draw the attention of Mrs. Igna, "is very interesting what your daughter said," Igna answered, "Yes, I do not know what is wrong with that girl's mind, we will see if one day she can compose or get some common sense." No, the nun answered, her daughter does not think like the rest of the children of her age, she thinks in the future. Ana then continued, "I'd be like you, a Messenger of God when I get educated. And will teach people who don't know how to live." The nun smiled and said "surely someday you will..." later she left.

Mrs. Igna had a problem understanding Ana's behavior, she speculated that maybe when Ana hit her head while running instead of walking, she probably caused some damage when walked on uneven surface and fell hitting the ground with her forehead . As a consequence of falling, Ana had done everything "different", she had learned to talk before walking, walk without crawling and instead of baby 'steps, she would stood up and ran. But it never occurred to the lady that physical and mental abuse also makes the children to change their behavior for better or for worse. Mrs. Igna just thought that probably if she engendered another girl would probably "would come out" better than Ana. So she began to work in her "new project" and it was easier "said and done", so she became pregnant in a "blink of an eye". The odd case was that she said that she had many "boys" by accident, but that it always wanted to have "the girl of her dreams," that was something that Ana could not understand.

A few months after that conversation, the pregnancy of the lady was quite noticeable. And Igna said she was pregnant with a "baby girl", according to her wish, thus this time she wasn't so moody like in the other pregnancies. But, for good or bad luck, -sometimes things happen for a reason-, so one fine day don Ira was in the cornfield (milpa) he had not many people who could help him, so he sent an acquaintance—who was passing by- to his home with a donkey loaded with sacks of corn. The man went directly to Ira's home but did not unloaded the donkey. As he was "in a hurry", Mrs. Igna noticed, that the donkey appeared tired and she tried to unloaded it herself. Big mistake! When she untied the bulk, she let it rest on her belly, and the fetus could not handle it. The Lady began to feel "labor pains" and she then looked for help. It was too late! The lady suffered a "miscarriage." And to make matters worse, it was a girl that could had been born! According to Igna. But she could not make the connection of how "things happen for a reason."

THE PROLIFERATION TO AVOID LOSING THE PRACTICE

To avoid losing practice, a few months later Igna was pregnant again, but this time she was already resigned to do it, since family planning brigades, educational pamphlets, or the radio propaganda approaches of "small family lives better" did not serve as much. It appeared that instead of stopping proliferation, the "family planning" administrated more fertilizer. It didn't matter that the kids were rebellious, always hungry, sleep on the floor, or were filled with lice and parasites and lived in a hostile environment; nothing stopped Ana's parents from their task of having all the children that the body could produce.

Months later the following baby was born, and as Igna suspected it was another "machito" boy. By then the idea of "the blonde girl with blue eyes" had vanished. So the only thing that was left was to accept what it came. The baby was not "white," but looked "exactly as his father" said a family's friend. And because it was brown "morenito" it had more resistance to disease, and did not get sick easily or at least it recovered faster than the whites "gueritos", since they were more delicate according to his mother, and to her it didn't matter if it was a boy because it was worth just for being his favorite.

Shortly before 2 years, the next baby was born, but this time was born white "guerito" to the delight of the parents, the curious thing about the boy was that being white came out malnourished and very frail. His skin look white as the snow, it was hard to know if it was yellow, pale or if only was his natural whiteness. It also had very black hair and a "tuft of reeds" on the left side of the head, with small but very black eyes. Igna did not care much about being malnourished, but she could make him feel better with affection calling him "Chabela chegunda" referring to the Queen "Elizabeth II." And as the very bottom of her fantasy she wanted it to be girl according to her dreams. Igna passed much of her time entertained with the new boy... Meanwhile Ana was in charge of caring for the rest of the kids. As with the newborn Igna had no time for the others.

But the picture was not complete, since the "guerito" didn't develop as easily as the rest of the kids. Concerned the lady decided to read brochures of nutrition that the social workers or health educators left for the "family planning." They said mothers had to start trying to feed the babies with other meals as early as three months old, so that they were developing their taste for meals and eventually learn to eat "adult food." As the Lady didn't have much logic, she took a bottle of milk, added a raw egg and stick it to the baby. The next day she noticed that the baby was getting some color, but it was red color because he could not defecate. She thought that at last the baby was "grabbing some color."

Another day went by and the baby was not red anymore instead he turned "purple" because it could not "make a poop". The "comadre" and other ladies suggested remedies, such as *"enemas"* so that the baby boy could have a bowel movement. Seeing that they didn't have big effect, they thought that the solution was to pray and mourn. Maybe he would die, "what a shame as cute as he was" the ladies said. It was the fourth day and the baby did not stop crying, then Ana told the ladies, maybe he needs to get checked by the doctor. Perhaps the doctor could do something to make him defecate. They look at Ana like as she got "two heads" and said "go girl until you said something meaningful."

The next day the Lady left the village with her little ill baby to see the doctor, for the baby was almost out of energy to weep. Ana was in charge of the rest of the kids as usual. It was good for her according to her mother, so she also had to learn how to cook, it was "that simple" or they starve to death. Meanwhile the Lady tried to save her "guerito." The mother returned the next day with the already cured "guerito." The doctor had made him something that helped him defecate, and had recommended to the lady to take good care of him since she nearly lost it due to the time that it took to seek care. That became beyond mother's comprehension since in her mind she had the idea that if one die could be "replaced" by another soon. But luckily the baby boy was saved so they continued the tradition and Don Ira thought that his lineage was dispersing, according to his idea of life.

THE REPRODUCTION CONTINUES

Not missing a beat, months later Igna was pregnant again. Don Ira, said "It is good" "God gives children to those who deserves them." Ana watched the scene and felt as if she and her siblings were sinking into a dead-end and bottomless well. How was possible that someone would think on having more children in that environment so bleak and depressing? Why her parents thought it could be approved as ideal to live? Ana's parents had no idea of what their children were suffering. Furthermore, they did not worry, because the cradle for the new born was ready year after year, whenever they brought a new baby to the world, the previous one went to sleep on the floor and they had to survive the cold and the hardness of it since life was not "easy" for anyone.

Ana was trying to distract herself from that scenario, she listened to songs for children and lullabies as the ones composed by Don "CriCri" among the favorites were "Mrs. Duck" and the "three little pigs." The latter said "the little pigs are already in bed, many good night kisses mother had given, and cozy and warm (calientitos) all in pajamas, in a while the three will snore (roncaran)..." Ironically what Ana observed was much different, Ana and her siblings slept on the uneven hard and dusty floor on a mat broken and smelly, covered with pieces of old and dirty blankets. While the parents slept in bed with thick mattress springs, covering with blankets that although stinky were newer to the ones their children had, and apart were plush and warm. But parents were oblivious of the misery lived by their children and even if they did know, it seemed they knew how to hide it quite well, since they never slept on the floor.

As life continued, the couple (senores) were enduring the task of proliferating, for them there was no point of return to "normality" because they were already poor and ignorant, and "had to endure the rod"–as the condemn do- and life will go on. Harvests were even scarcer, since the times of drought continued. Sometimes there was no water on the well and people would fight to get a list a few drops of "clean" water at least to drink, and for other needs Ana had to bring the water from the creek to boil since it was dirty. In order to survive, the ladies were fighting for a bucket of clean water from the well as it no longer produced water. Ana had to wake up before sunrise, when it was still dark in the morning to bring a little water to drink for the whole family and get confronted by older people who were trying to get some clean water too.

Ana began to feel ill and she did not know if it was weakness or stress or both. She had some white spots all over the body and the white part of the eye was yellow. The aunt Lolita tried to cure Ana with her usual remedies but they made no effect. She had "upset stomach" and didn't want to eat beans with "weevils" that was the only thing they had. Her parents were no much worried about the fact that Ana did not want to eat since others could get better portions, and said that "among less donkeys more cobs," what really worried them was that she could not work as fast as it did before. So one fine day they took her to the doctor for the first time in her life. The response of doctor was that Ana was very anemic, and prescribed some pills and recommended to eat "meat" Ana then felt as if someone had brought her afloat, "red meat" was what she wanted he most, but it was only a "dream" since the family ate meat only when someone at the ranch decided to kill a bull or when they were shot in the ravines or ditch and found them on good time to eat them.

Months later, Ana had survived the anemia, Mrs. Inga started with her aches or pains and "bad mood." To Ana that was not new, Igna her mother, was pregnant again. Don Ira was very happy and said, at last there is "good news," probably this bring us better luck. Thus, it was born the next son of the "happy couple." This came out brown "prietito" but at least was a boy "little man." But did not have nothing under his arm, as they expected him to have – la torte- the sandwich under his arm, since people said that there was no reason to worry about the new born since most of the kids were born with their fate under the arm. And as the Lady still dreamed of "a girl" she called him my "negrita" –my little brown- many years later he would give them a surprise, but not to transform into a girl, because although it wasn't "little woman" had other trends that the "couple" had never though that could happen to them.

After the rejoice of the new born, it occur to Ana's parents that provisions were already quite scarce, don Ira had noticed that there was not much more to do, so he went to look for work outside the ranch. Leaving the Lady with a lot of little kids and almost nothing to eat. Although it was very common to see Igna's face of hopeless, this time the "Lady" had a countenance of sadness and desolation, at that situation she was seen much more worried than usual. And as- the gossips were never missing-, because they said that it did not matter that Igna gave a bunch of kids "chamacos" to don Ira, since he had left her anyways... As the account of the credit with the little convenience store –tiendita- was already running out, Igna told Ana that they had to eat a tortilla with a tomatillo salsa that she had collected from the field. While the children had to settle with soup of beans and tortilla pieces because not even the hens could lay eggs.

One day don Ira returned from his trip. He had managed to work a bit and gather some money, however due to the debt with the convenience store (tiendita) during his absence, after paying the shopkeeper, he was left with no much to survive. After learning the experience now Ana's parents realized that they had complicated life, finally had realized that even though they denied it, "the small family lives better" particularly in those times of crisis. But rather than accept that educators were right, Don Ira said "hunger is bad, but worst is that one who endure it." And according to Don Ira, if someone complained it was because it was a coward… Ana observed everything that happened with caution, because if questions were asked, her parents would scold or punished her.

Despite everything that was happening, Don Ira did not want to leave his lands. Although some people had suggested to him that it was best to go to the city, he didn't want to stop working the plot, which was not productive any more, even for the most indispensable needs, and even rain was not helping by what the land was already sterile. Many people had acknowledged the situation and had already left the Ranch to go to the city to seek a new life that would give them at least for the basics. The Government did not know how to deal with so much emigration from the farms to the cities and implemented "orientation programs." For the peasant, invented songs that made them think as "a farmer wept" and others to discourage them not to move to the city, since they knew that more people in the city made the crisis worst.

Don Ira got very thoughtful when listening to the song "a farmer wept" and also tears of sadness came out of his eyes, although he said that "males don't cry." Also he began to think that he had to work for others when he had been self-employed for many years. As the crisis continued worsening, poor Don Ira at least now was contemplating the possibility of going to the city. Don Ira saw the eight kids sickly and malnourished and thought that the universe had been conspired against him. Ana contemplated the depressing situation, however knowing her father, the possibility to get out of it was very remote. Even suicidal thoughts came to her mind, if father did not take the decision out of that misery, then it was not worth living. But as her mind had too much logic, she had to think about it more than once.

Ana analyzed different options and thought about the possibilities of that with her bad luck, probably if attempt was not successful, but she end up crippled would be even worse, because now it would be one burden to the family. Also as no one "gave a poop" it did not mattered what she thought or did, maybe if her attempt worked, nobody would be benefited from it , and on the contrary what they would think it would be that "as fewer donkeys more cobs" and siblings could eat a crumb of which corresponded to her as part of the clan. On the contrary of the suicidal idea, came up with praying for -the Almighty- to do something for the family and granted her a miracle out of that so depressing place. Then a miracle happened, suddenly someone arrived from the city. After long conversations, they tried to convince Don Ira that it was best for the family to go to the city. A man would get him a job in a factory, and once he already have some money could come to pick up the kids if they survive from hunger and famine... Ana could not believe that her prayers had been answered and then thought that God had not abandoned her. When she arrived at the city she would go to the Church to give thanks to the Lord.

As a result of so much stress, Ana had many dreams and nightmares, among them dreamed that she fell into a bottomless abyss and that she could not touch the bottom. She also dreamed that she would be crossing the river and suddenly sliding rocks made her fell into the cold water. Another dream was that black, big dogs attacked her and she had to destroy them in pieces. When the hope began to flourish in her mind, also dreams began to change, because she had more control over them, now when she fell into the abyss she could seize the grasses surrounding the well, and if she failed she would continue to sleep and as not touching bottom woke up in the middle of the fall. As for dogs, she would be prepared and when they were nearby she would cut into their head with a giant pair of scissors or a giant knife. She could also control take-offs of the soul, when the soul abandoned her during those nights of intense cold that reached her bones and that nearly left her unconscious. Which also caused her pains (rheumatic pain) during most of the winter…

A few weeks later the remote idea of moving to the city came more alive, Don Ira decided finally to go and give it a try to a job in the city. Later, a letter to Mrs. Igna arrived from the city, Don Ira told her that the relatives had gotten him to work in a factory and that he had already a place to live. The news could not be better; to Ana, that represented a complete change, at least "the Lady" would stop complaining about her "destiny." Probably in that unknown place there was food to eat and Ana would not have to see the face of her brothers when they were hungry after the small portions that they had to eat. Life could not be "so cruel" as that one she had lived on the ranch full of ignorant poor people and with bad vibe that they made her get sick just by being close to her. Now the environment would be more promising since at least people had to eat in that distant and unknown place according to Ana's dream for the whole family.

After packing their (tiliches) the few belongings that they had, the family was ready and waiting for Don Ira to come and take the family to a new place. The days seemed eternal, but at last the awaited day came. After negotiating the small house Ira had built with so "much sacrifice," Don Ira said goodbye to the compadres and more people that they would continue back there trying to survive with what others left on their way to a better life. Ana did not understand why it hurt so much to Don Ira to leave that place so sad and dry. Only some giant trees such as Walnuts remained since the drought had ended with most of the greenery of the place. But Don Ira had made a promise that one day would return to have her own piece of land full of trees.

THE NOSTALGIA OF DEPARTING

Ana and her family were preparing to depart, the mixed feelings of departing to never come back were in the air, and Ana couldn't help feeling nostalgia for what was left behind. So many good and bad memories crowded her mind as a dramatic film. Between what had happened, she had calamities and hardships, and also some few good memories. How to forget the first House that her eyes saw, the patio, which divided the House used for sleeping and the kitchen. That great covered patio by the Bower that Ana had swept with that broom made of green thickets that filled her hands of calluses. Also how to forget the garden (Huerta) that was once very fertile with its pomegranates, peaches and apples. The lot that gave corn and Zucchini for soup in their good times. The plot which had been productive and that Ana and her siblings had been planted grains under the intense sun. The stream (creek) that fed the animals and also provided water to wash clothes for the family.

Who could forget those fresh mornings, but at the same time warm in summer? And the mornings of winter when the cold would get to the bones. The days of warm rain in the summer... And those cold and wet winter days that made her ill of rheumatism and made her cry. Forget the bucket of cooked corn (nixtamal) that she had to grind with the handle mill... Other thoughts that assaulted her mind was how in the world people were able to think that way of life was accepted by the others without protest. That lifestyle where nobody talked about love, happiness, or the fantasy or dream of a different worlds. Thus it was the ranch of the Saucito (The Willow) were only prevail lamentations and sorrows.

THE WILLOW AND THE LAMENTS

The Willow was the name of the village that housed Ana's family and other 13 families each with its own character. As the "weeping willow", families living inside of that small ranch also cried, complained and lamented what calamities they survived. Starting from the South side of the ranch, lived Doña Andite with her sons Tony and Kiko. Nobody ever saw her husband, probably she was a widow. The younger Tony was who supported the family, Kiko the oldest had already lost his mind and I didn't work, just walked through all the ranch rambling as if his mind were in another world. Neighbors said that a "bad woman" had made him witchcraft and she had left him so "crazy". No one could think that other things could have happened that if "Kiko" was suffering from mental illness. That was how that small family lived with their problem on their backs and praying to relieve their sorrows.

The second family was Neto and Pancracia who were cousins of the first family. They had 4 children alive but the people muttered that "the Lady" had lost several children because of "its witchcraft". They said -evil tongues- that Pancra practiced witchcraft to get rid of bad people who she did not like, that on full Moon days she wore ointments that made her invisible as well as her broom, and since she could not see with her own eyes, she borrowed it out of cats and looked better at night and who she would put a spell on, Pancra also knew how to "bring down" owls since they helped identify those who deserved the witchcraft. The children were not that bad, Tony had developed the ability to play the accordion, and played in the small parties of the ranch. His brother Nacho helped him playing guitar, so the two rehearsed every day in the evening after work everybody suspected there was a "party" coming. Lupe helped with the housework to Pancra, and the smallest was the shepherd of goats. That one was pretty wild, aside from using a vocabulary quite dirty when he talked with others, he was very rude with his classmates and a real headache for teachers. On one occasion he stole the savings that the students were giving to the teacher for the "mother's day." He would fight constantly with the other boys and girls and he would show his private parts to the girls to scare them. No one knew why he was so evil.

The following family was that of Felix, he was the "rich" (wealthy) of the ranch. People speculated that Felix had found a "pot" filled with gold coins. People told these stories in those outposts of civilization there were those who by luck or by accidents of life were able to have treasures, that rich people (farmers and landowners) had been hiding (buried) during the war against the revolutionaries... With the money from the "treasure" Felix had managed to put the "tendajo" a convenience store, he also bought fine cattle, and had a large family. He entertained the family with the "tendajo" and taught them the value of money. While he was in charge of negotiating their cattle, since Felix was the only one who had spotted cows "Charolaise" as well as pedigree bulls, and "Hertford." But people had no explanation of why he had a wife as "ugly and skinny," the most curious case is that they had a dozen children!

Felix always wore white nose caps, -since people said- that he had a rare disease due to the fact that when he had unburied the "treasure", he had not had time to cover the nose to avoid "gases or poison" and as a result they damaged his respiratory system, thereafter he would have to use "medicine" for the rest of his life. Interestingly enough, that had not prevented him from having a dozen kids with Petra his wife. Petra was a skinny and rough woman who never wore makeup, dressed in rags and was always barefoot. People never understood her behavior or had explanation for it. As Felix being a rich man, how he could not have found something "better," since men with money always chose the most beautiful women of the ranch.

But Felix didn't care to what people say. Somehow they had made a "great family". Lela was the oldest, colorless and thin as her parents, but the men besieging her for being a daughter of "Don Felix." But for his father, no man was worthy of having "Lela" so she ended up being "kidnapped" by one of her suitors. Mina was not so graceful, she was born with a "virolo eye" and was also skinny and full of "stains" in her face so she was easy going and not presumed anything. So she was very religious and liked to invite the kids from other families to walk the rain Saint "San Isidro". She adorned a chair with the photograph of the Holy

Saint and with a group of children walked into the different fields of corn (solar) singing "Lord San Isidro, revered Holy, your rain has given a nice planted..." Curiously for when the ritual ended, they began to feel the rain, and rained so hard that when all children returned home it was in full swing.

Lencho was the tendajo's attendant, but thus he hypothesized that "yes he knew how to make money" although he did not know anything else and tried to buy favors from the girls in the ranch, since he could not conquer anyone with personal appeal, for being ugly and tongue-tied attributes. Filo was also a stutterer and had a "foot throw" every time he walked he would throw the foot to the right before taking the next step. Chui and Elena were the most "normal" they were scholars of the family. Gulf was also good at school but was also stuttered. Pita, Crista, Chayo and others had still to boast about since they were very small girls and only were the daughters of "Don Félix." Since Felix bragged and wanted his family to be a model family, people "kept an eye" on them, therefore said that although he was "rich" not escaped from having children with defects since there was no "beauty without defect, nor ugly without grace" they also said that it was "easier to pass a camel through the hole of a needle as a 'rich' to enter into the Kingdom of heaven."

The following family was Bunio and Soco, they were two solitons (single) brothers who had left to spend a life of youth since they felt obligated to take care of their mother, who was suffering from an incurable disease. They were so quiet and submissive, because apart from being poor, they never went to school so they only had to work, eat and take care of the ailing mother. Poor lady lived in pain, because there was no day that people would not hear her moans through all the ranch. Some people said that the bones and joints hurt as if they were burning her on the inside, the hut where she asleep it stank horrible and said that the smell was due to the remedies that the curandero applied to her. No one knew the reason for her illness and people muttered that she had been punished for some unknown reason since even the best healers could not cure it. Poor children only prayed that someday she will stop suffering. For years the old woman suffered its penalty, until death or a good day God took pity of her and died. Soco and Bunio, were those adult children who survived on memories of her moans, who had only poverty and desolation they felt in that family and now they only had to pray that they did not have the same destiny.

The following "almost family" was Uncle Tolo and his son Beto. They lived alone, but it was not always that way. Said people that knew them from before, that Uncle Tolo was married once and that because he did not like to work as he had sought someone who support him. Apparently he was "handsome", or at least had a good presence -he thought that he was coming from superior race from (Spain)-. So he had sought a wife Keita (who was not very beautiful) who had no pity on the idea of support him. With luck he had found one, so even if she wasn't so pretty she had accepted "the deal" to support him.

They said,- those who knew her- that she was "very luchona" hard worker and that apart from attending her husband, she made tortillas to sell to other people so she could get some income , she also survived washing and laundering for the neighbors, and raised chickens and turkeys, sold eggs and chicks and coconitos for those who would buy them. Apart she had giving a child to tio Tolo so he could be entertained with. The son Beto inherited his father in the laziness and without any grace or beauty, so both relied on (pobrecilla) Lady to support them. Beto was slow so to speak, and people didn't know if it was slow of birth or if it was just pure laziness. To make matters worse it was quite ugly also, that was people said.

An unexpected day the poor wife of the tio Tolo fell ill and died. People said that she had probably fallen ill on her lungs of working so hard for both lazy men. So were there were two "homeless" to the "good grace of God." As neither of them knew anything and neither wanted to do anything, when hunger was attacking them, they would go to beg food with residents of the ranch. Most of the people got used or accustomed to seeing them almost always come at lunch time or dinner. Sometimes they were lucky and they ate more than once but then got indigested "se empachaban."

Thus they lived for many years, and as the two were useless and the tio Tolo already had become (feito) ugly as his son, so no one could thought about marriage. One day Uncle Tolo became ill by "an old ache" to those who felt pity for him went to see what they could do for him, unfortunate "the evil illness" was already very advanced. It was "raving" between roars and vomiting, he called on people that they did not let him die, because he wanted to continue living and "keep eating." Even with all the sorrows and ravings uncle Tolo had the desire to live, although it was on charity of others. So finally Uncle Tolo died, leaving her son Beto helpless and without any tools in order to survive. Beto continue begging for favors and food between residents and died a few months later without saying "water goes". People grumbled that his father had sympathized with him and had "brought it" with him to where he was "God knew where."

The unique Bachelor of all the ranch was don Delfi, and no one knew why he had chosen to live alone. When someone had dared to ask why, he always gave different versions. One of them was that women made him sick since they were very "filthy." And also some gossips said that it was because he was very stingy or disliked neither men nor women. He lived in his garden with all kinds of fruit trees and they were his way of making his living. Rarely someone would visited him either. Sometimes just to have some contact with the others he would threw some apples to children who passed only to draw a little attention. Delfi had decided to be his own family by himself.

The following family was formed of Vito and Pablito (Paul). They were a very unique couple, Vito was hardly four feet of height. While Pablito her husband, was more than six feet tall. Vito had never learned to read and write (she was very illiterate), but spoke more than a frightened parrot (crazy cacatua). She loved to gossip and lived to visit neighbors and talk about them as it was "the newspaper" of "alarm" on the ranch. No one knew how she had time to be a "house wife" and been given 8 children to Pablito nor how it had understood Pablito's proposal. Pablito was also illiterate and hardly spoke to any one and when he talked to someone he would talk in a very slow tone. Pablito used to walk slowly but with big step since it was very tall. Vito said that although she was chubby and had a waist of hen, she had not always been that chubby and blamed Pablito for having made her have so many children! Between their 8 children excelled their two older daughters who surely helped to support the family.

Chuya was the oldest who helped Vito with the other kids, but as it was not enough since she grew up a little more, she flew to the city to work as a maid and could contribute to support the House. Eventually she married, but by then the next sibling was ready to work (fight for the survival of the home), she had grown and apart from working hard at home, it was her turn to bring money into the House. When it was her turn to marry, there was another in training. Lupe was the next on the list, so she also dedicated herself to be maid but she was even "more noble". Soon she became the heroine of the family because she supported not only her parents but was also responsible for the two younger kids who she tried so hard to get them out of ignorance.

Lupe wanted those younger siblings no to suffer her hardship for what had happened to her by hard work, and so she wanted the two male brothers, May and Hetor, to study and become teachers. While the youngest Mary, she would become a "Secretaria". With thousands of sacrifices Lupe became their sponsor and pushed them to study hard to eventually pay back for their studies. Unfortunately, their IQ did not help much, and so it did not matter how much support they had, they could not "keep up" with the responsibility since "the books" were too much for them. Even though tried in good will they never could graduate as teachers. And Mary, never was able to complete her career nor since the shorthand could not record in her mind and was very slow for typing. What else could they expect coming from two illiterate parents?

Another peculiar family was the family of don Bucho. He had a family that was not mixed with anyone, people only saw them when attending an event at the ranch, or when they were in the bus as passengers to the nearest town. To protect his family don Bucho had surrounded its solar (parcel) of nopales (cactus) as protection so that no one approached his daughters or try to bother him. No one knew if he had a wife or not since he was the only one who came to bring what the family needed. And it was not so friendly so what happened inside of "the nopalera" was a mystery.

The number ten family was the family of Cleo and Conra. Although their names were crossed they were or wanted to be happy in their own world. His name was derived from "Cleopatra" Cleo and his wife derived from a man name "Conrad." He was skinny and chaparrito (short) while she was still more chaparrita and skinnier than him. The men of the ranch said (muttered) he had fathered tiny girls as the only children they could have for being so chaparritos (hobbits). They had fathered 7 children and a "gingerbread boy" chaparrito. The oldest was skinny and tiny girl, her neglecting mother had taken her out in the cold while was very hot inside the home and the impact of the cold air had deviated her eye so the poor girl saw with a deviated eye and that was her shame. The next was the "little boy" that was spoiled as a brat, they care for him as it if were made of gold, since it was the only one they could have; also was chaparrito and had a tiny brain. The following girl was very cute like a little doll (curiosita blanquita) she strove much to get good grades, very blonde but sometimes came to the class with the lice which she tried to hide with the glitter her mother put on the hair.

Then it was Maru, the poor thing was born less white than the others and therefore the mother made her feel less. Then Paquita her younger sibling was very white as a plastic doll. Maru had fallen ill of anemia, since mother did not fed her well or cared for her, like she did for others for the simple fact of "being brown". Conra did not care much to cure her because she was very pregnant. Instead they gave her only left overs and although the poor thing was consumed slowly by her illness, it seemed like no one cared, but she was yellow and limply just lying on her small bed. The day of giving birth was coming and Conra had to stay in bed since she was "very fragile". So mother and daughter were confined to their own beds. One day Maru did not arise from her small bed, her tired body had perished. Interestingly enough, her mother Conra gave birth the next day to another girl to whom she registered with the same name "in her honor" Conra said that life and God had provided a "spare" as chickens are replaced. For a change the new baby had come out very similar to the one just passed away, but now they would care for her because even when she was brunette it was only meant to be.

Family number 11 was the family of Beto and Rey. And they were no two men thus lady was called Rey. Beto was the eldest son of don Greg, although his father was a hardworking, Beto was not as smart as his father, the only thing he had inherited him was a taste for making children since it also had a lot of little kids. Although the gossipy people said that with the help of "one or another volunteer". Rey had no close family or at least nobody knew her a relative. She said she was "Christian" aka "sister." She said that "brothers" helped with food, money and clothing so she did not worry if she continued giving birth to many children "left and right." The oldest daughters were Elvia and Nicky, they looked like twins since they were almost a year's apart. They were in charge of caring for the kids for a while until they were more developed and went to the city to work of servants or workers. Then followed Geno, Blas and Cesar, feitos (ugly and evil) – they were "wild" since they had no education and "didn't know manners" because they were shepherds of goats and did not like the school.

Beto the father of the kids was not so ugly, so the people grumbled that the kids had went ugly because maybe someone "had eaten his groceries" (meaning he was not the father of those kids), but poor Beto was not angry he was shy and only "turned red". Rey used to take off from home whenever her husband wasn't enough to give for the expenditure. Suddenly there was Rey taking a bath, then she wore her best clothes and make up and her perfume, and came out to the road where passing truckers drove, who she called for "a ride" since she had no money. The truckers went to the nearest town with the company of Rey. The next day she was returning well served, with several bags of food and other items.

When talked to the neighbors of her adventure, she said "thanks God who never deprive me anything..." and "extended" her (breast up) chest and straighten the back and sticking out her butt. And so the days passed until then she noticed that she was pregnant again. When gave birth this time she had twins (cuates.) The girl came out brunette as Rey but the boy came out with hazel eyes and fair skin. The neighbors said that at least this time Rey had chosen well who had paid the "favor". The poor Beto only turned his "face on colors" with the hurtful comments of others. And so it continued her work Rey until she completed the dozen. With help or without help, Beto could not get a "break" at all… Well, the ugly boys continued without major change, later they left to continue their "job" in the big city. One of the daughters became exhibitionist and was "making out" as bride and groom in some spots of the ranch, while the other sister left "disappeared," people said that she got pregnant and married in some faraway place.

Family number 12 were the Herrera, who were far apart from the rest of the people. They were as three families in one since lived very near each other. The mother of all of them was an elderly lady who looked very different to the rest of the neighbors, she had long black hair but very fair (white) skin, very different from others. People grumbled that she was a "White Witch" was also the midwife to some deliveries of the women from the ranch. Tella and the Guera, were her youngest daughters they were very nice and no one dared to disrespect them, because they said that the mother could do witchcraft if someone dare to do so. At home there were only adults since for some reason they liked to work hard and had plots that produced them good harvests and also had many cows. And if someone was daring to trespassing, their gun was ready for them in case someone would try to "mess" with their animals or sisters. The Lady mother Gina was very delicate seemed like not the same breed of others of the ranch. They said that probably had Spanish blood and so had other habits. She was very different from the "witch Pancra" in the South of the ranch, but also knew her spells. Truth or lie she not churned lot with the riff-raff of the ranch.

Family number 13 was the family of Tita. She was the healer of the ranch, she had three children, Mago, Tota and Nana. Tita had been left widow of very young age, with three creatures to raise. But she had devoted to several trades, she was the healer of the ranch, also knew how to make griddles, made tortillas to the ladies who paid to help them, and also wrote letters for the illiterate who wanted to communicate with their families, but who couldn't read or write. With great sacrifice she had raised her three sons. When Mago grew up he got assigned a parcel and so he could support his sisters and his mother Tita, then Tota and Nana went to the city to work as maids in wealthy houses and thus contributed to the expenses of the House. After working for several years they got married and formed their own families. Later on Mago also got a girl and brought her to live with his mother Tita.

THE FAMILY MODEL

Family number 14, was the family of Don Ira and Doña Igna, a couple with a long history of "love of tragic-comedy" (that will be later narrated). They also had a large family as controversial as the beginning of their life as a couple. Ana was the daughter they had never dream of. She was born in mid-summer with the Sun as her star and planet regent and the element of fire as the basis of her life. She had opened her eyes as soon as she was born, (feature no so common in those days). Apart from opening the eyes, she also watched carefully to all who approached her cradle. And to make it more complicated to her parents, she began to speak sooner than to walk. She never crawl and liked to be sitting instead, but one fine day she stood up and began to walk and then run, regardless of how many times she fell on that uneven and cobbled floor, she would continue running.

Ana observed the dynamics of what happened around her carefully, as if she wanted to read through the mind of anyone who surrounded her. When something seemed totally rare for her, she did not hesitate to ask and scrutinize the smallest detail. She wondered what would have happened really to "Kiko loco," whether Pancra was really a "witch" or why her son "Bocho" was so bad (evil) that everyone was afraid of him in the ranch. Another question that Ana entertained in her mind was, why the painful disease of the mother of Soco and Bunio, and the contrast of the good luck of Felix (the wealthy) the wealthy of the ranch, and if he actually found a "treasure."? How could be possible that only a few meters away from Felix, lived the tio Tolo (uncle) and his son Beto who never had food to eat and they never worked or did anything in their life? Why Delphi was not married or formed a family and what was the mystery of living alone? Why Vito spoke so much —like a cacatua- and was illiterate, as she could have 8 children and didn't work either? That mystery locked in the family of Don Bucho? Why the Herrera did not mingled with anyone but nevertheless people respect them? Mrs. Gina was a "White Witch" or they just said that because she looked different from the rest of the ladies? What would have happened to the husband of aunt Tita and why she was so hard worker "luchona" and always had a face of sadness and desolation?

Ana was overwhelming her parents with questions and thoughts. Her parents don Ira and Doña Igna had no patience or answers for so much curiosity. So rather than complicate their life, they had decided to punish her whenever she asked something that did not seem to them to be "normal." Also they had decided that since she did not meet the characteristics that they waited in their offspring, so they had to use her dynamism and put it to work as a "maid" to see if she would change. As part of the punishment was, to break her "ego" minimizing her self-esteem and ridiculing her way of behaving. Apart from forcing her to do "adult work" and avoid contact with the neighborhood children so she would not take more ideas of what she already had. So they limited her to play with all kinds of games, toys, and any kind of privilege that any girl her age could have deserved. And on top of it, they limited her food, made her sleep on the floor and beat her constantly, leaving marks on her legs so if she escaped from home to go to school the marks would cause her shame when classmates teased her about it. What Ana's parents never imagined was that she had been born with a self-determination that was uncommon in those days; for Ana no obstacle would minimize her force to live. Any one could say that it applied the phrase "That which doesn't kill you makes you stronger." And thus, Ana grew until one day she had the courage to break the chains that tied her to that family and left.

The next son of Don Ira and Doña Igna was "the boy of their eyes," since he was born as they had wished it, a boy of fair skin and curly hair which came from his mother, they could not ask for more to life! Just had a tiny problem, he was too sensitive to the sun and every time he was exposed to it, he was bleeding through the nose under the blazing sun of summer. But rather than punish him as they did with Ana, it provoked them shame and pity and they sent Ana to end the task of seeding in the corn field. Curiously Ana's head also hurt but she would recover more easily. So it grew up the "Chino" as they called him and became "a playboy" of the neighborhood, and as they allowed him to do what he wanted because it was regarded "like a rooster" and conqueror, he said that he had "knocked down" more than one girl pregnant. And as vain thought he was untouchable, when he was getting ready to get married became ill in such a way that did not see the end of it (he thought it was a spell). He consulted with a doctor and a "White Witch" to make a clean (cleanse), probably his consciousness tormented him since also he had "predicted" to Ana that she would come out with "a baby out of wedlock" or pregnant before marriage, even though she did not have a boyfriend and was too busy going to school and working. With the passing of time the law of "karma" charged posturing of his youth. And 20 years later his precious daughter (17y/o) made his prophecy come true, got very pregnant by the teacher since it was closer and did not want to look for more.

The next kid was the white "Guero," also cared so much by the parents because he had been born "weakling", they assigned the name of "Angel" because they thought it was a miracle that had not been aborted by Igna; since due to a "fright sickness" caused by her brother who came -one day in the middle of the night- bleeding due to a stub he had suffered in a fight., Igna almost abort out "guero" ahead of time. Anyway, this was not the only shock given by the "guero," to make matters worse he came out listless and sickly. It was not developed as they expect it, it took him too much of effort to turn himself in his own crib. It was exactly the opposite of Ana. He almost died according to Doña Igna, but was saved by "a magical healer" who gave him his life back. It took him a long time to return to normal development, he even confused the "pop" of his diaper with food and ate when her mother took time to change it. Followed between missteps and lack of character all his life, grew a bit, fell in love with women like him. And then drank constantly to forget who he was and how it would solve the problems.

The next child was Sam "the replacement." It was almost a year's difference with guero because Igna had conceived it thinking that if guero did not survive, they had their replacement. So the poor Sam didn't know why they despised him and did not receive the care given to the guero, unconsciously he had developed the idea that he would survive no matter what others say or think, so he did not give a "cumin" -%$#@- the opinion of others, as a baby he used to finish his bottle and take the bottle of guero to satiate his hunger then when he could walk he escaped to the house of Tita to ask for a taco since it was not filled with the portion given by Igna. Don Ira was trying to make him work harder than the guero because he was stronger, though he was skinny and malnourished, but wasn't as sickly and "quejambroso" wining as guero. Thus Sam grew up caring less for education never was ashamed when he showed his grades or report card full of "red fives" he said that they were an ornament for his card and did not cared for the scolding of don Ira. When he became adult used to say to the rest of the family that he was "neutral" and that he knew that was his life. After 35 y/o he started to get grey hair and thought it was time to find a woman to form what he called a "happy" family.

The next son of Don Ira and Igna was "Tuito." It seemed that they had made him with hot pepper "chili piquin." Since baby Tuito was a real "headache." He cried day and night for the slightest reason. He beat the crib against the wall until he fell to the ground and then began to cry at the door entrance until someone could rescue him. And if he was mad about someone or something he would make a big temper-tantrum so he would crawl towards the closest wall and crashed his head against it, but if the wall was very far it dropped his head on the ground in protest. On one occasion when his mother put him in the arms of Ana so she had to hold him, he burst in a temper tantrum and twisted as a worm, Ana could not control him, and the little boy slipped from Ana's arms and fell into the ashes and coals. His mother punished Ana and then it made sure that el Tuito was not burned, luckily nothing happened to the kid. To remove a little anger of the rebellious child they had to take him to see "San Francisco de Asís,"- Francis of Assisi- what calmed him down a little as his parents thought. With beating and scolding they controlled him until don Ira got tired. Unfortunately another crisis of adolescence reverted his rebelliousness, but as don Ira had already thought, Ana had to come to the rescue. Between conversations and shame he managed out of the bad steps he walked. And one day married and calmed himself again, thanks to life that a good woman touched his heart since probably that was what he needed, that arrangement would take him out of the risk of repeating the chain of rebellion and abuse.

Poncho was the next morenito in the family, whom by good luck was not as rebellious as his older brother, by then don Ira was already tired of beating the children, so Poncho did not receive the treatment as his older siblings did. He did not feel the belt marks on his skin. Therefore he could develop another vision of life.–although generics are hard to hide- He liked to sing, so they allowed him to go to the streets to sing like bird when he was only 5 years old, thus, he thought he was special (enlighten). So it was how his good fortune began, since his steps led him towards a kindergarten which was a few blocks from home. Poncho sang a song to the Director of the kindergarten, who caused her much grace and curiosity. Later she went to talk to the parents and asked them permission so that child could attend the first year of kindergarten. She would take care of all expenses as his parents did not have the payment fee or study material. Poncho was the only family member who attended kindergarten. What helped him to further develop his "intellectual skills". He earned first place on scores of elementary school and as a prize he got to travel to several important States in the country. He also had the privilege that his parents attended his graduations, since not all his brothers had that privilege. He eventually completed his College degree, and got a wife and formed a family with two children who he loves and thinks that they are the "little enlightened."

Key was the next in the family of 8 boys. He was born white as "milk" with a tuft of reeds or grey hair and eyes black as the night. Doña Igna was mesmerized with the newborn, because apart from being "blanquito" it was very quiet, even to cry was calm. Once got very sick because Igna made him eat a raw egg in the bottle of milk and caused him to get extremely constipated, he almost died -poor boy- of indigestion, but he escaped by the faith. After, he grew up a little he forgot who gave him the food that made him sick to death. A few years later, Igna used to forget to feed him and he pulled her skirt reminding her that he was missing to be feed. Thus he grew up and as irony graduated from "communication." But as we must not trust much of the calm and silent –harmless-, the family grew and scattered, he stayed to live free in the house that others had built, and bought another house and rented it. And to finish the tale he did not married to not "waste."

Huicho was the next in the remained in the string of little kids. He was born in times of "crisis." When it was not rain it was the great draught, there was no water, the land had become sterile,–which was not the case with the ladies of the ranch-, and to make matters worse his parents were already tired from everything and everyone. The poor kid was morenito –brown- his mother did not care much about the "morenito" thus, she didn't pay him much attention. On one occasion she did not want to wake up in the middle of the night to give him "pats on the back" to burp after feeding him and he almost died of indigestion; the good news was that she had Ana's help so she woke her up at 3:00 in the morning so she could help to care for the child. Ana was all sleepy took the baby in her arms, she was afraid that the child could die, and noted that his eyes were going blank and the body was lose, was then that it occurred to Ana to give him a few pats on the back. The baby boy then vomited a lot, his mother gave a Chamomile tea so he could fall asleep. Years later it was noticeable that his eye deviating whenever he fell sick. No one bother of checking the problem. As Inga always had the idea of girl in her mind called the poor Huicho "mi negrita"-black- being the morenito (brown) in the family. Thus the morenito grew up and although he didn't have much to be creative, years later graduated from the University. Then to honor his parents he introduced the "partner" to them, since he decided that women were not for him. That was a great surprise for his mother who always wanted "a girl", and for his father who was very proud of "manliness" of children who "God" had given him as a "reward" for being Don Ira.

Rafi, the youngest of the family, was the pylon –extra- and for a change, he was the spoil/favorite of the parents for being blondie "light-haired" and even if they did not wish to do so, the last to shut down the production of children. The Cherub was born in the city, was the only one who was born in a hospital bed. And although the Doña was already tired and completely worn out herself, she wanted to continue to the end. The doctor had suggested her to stop having children to la Doña, since she had lost all the teeth from lack of calcium, had pain in bones and joints, and she had to cut her long hair to be able to retain the calcium in her body. As a favor the doctor had tried to make it a "tie-down" when the Cherub was born but she had awakened during the attempt and ran away from the operating table. Months later and with the "push" of the family, finally the lady decided to stop the babies 'production.

The Cherubim then became the dearest treasure of Lady Igna. So she devoted herself to take care of it and take pictures to decorate the house like a gallery. As if it were the only son that she had given birth to. The cherub was the only one who drank milk, he was spoiled –as a brat-, Igna bought him his first bike, and a pet. He was the only one who did not sleep on the floor, as Ana who slept for 12 years in the soil since did not deserve a decent bed. For being so spoiled the kid did not developed much of his intellect, but according to his mother that didn't matter, since by being so "cute", he would find a woman who would not mind to support him financially, since she would picked up a keeper "wonderful man." Interestingly enough, the Cherub found a woman with much honor "honor to support him" and thus formed the Cherubim's family.

Don Ira, wanted a big family, also had his own story. He was the youngest of a family of 8 as he said. Apparently, when he was young, he had other brothers, they met none of their children, since they had died at the hands of gunmen who were enemies of the family due to quarrels of the ancestors. Ira was the youngest, and this helped him to survive since he would still growing up and was ignored just for being a child. He had 3 sisters who had married young and had left him only with his ailing mother. Therefore the circumstances had "forced" him to search for a woman who "would take care of him." Don Ira did not feel that he was ready to marry at age 25, but the situation impelled him to "procure" a companion.

THE BEGINNING OF THE ORDEAL

So Ira was observing his surroundings checking on girls and "selecting" who would be "the one" and –bingo- founded Doña Igna the youngest daughter of Don Greg. To whom he started courting unbeknown to her father, who jealously guarded the reputation of his daughters. Don Greg, father of Igna, he was a man of great respect and wanted his daughters to find a good husband who at least was hardworking, honest, and intelligent, since being wealthy was not easy in that poor Ranch. But the poor Don Ira, only needed a woman who "would take care of him" and he had (high expectations) putting his eyes on the younger daughter of Don Greg. Don Ira just had that "needs." So he had convinced Miss. Igna that although he did not have money, he had love and good intentions for her. And that living with him she would not be missing 'anything." After some affectionate letters Don Ira had convinced the young lady that he was the man that she needed to supplement her life.

Doña Igna, on the other hand, did not have much experience with "the outside world," since Don Greg only let out his daughters with chaperone if he would letting them go out for parties. As Don Greg provided them with the basics he hoped that when they marry, at least the husband fulfilled their basic needs. Don Greg's customs were very conservative because he belonged to a Spaniard's family who had lost everything they had during the time of the 1910 Revolution and Don Greg had to survive only with his intelligence and hard work. But Doña Igna for being the youngest of the daughters, have lacked herself out of appreciation, since what she resented the most –according to her- was the love from her mother who died when she was still a baby. Thus, she was only interested in fulfill her emptiness of affection. As a result she though that the affection of Don Ira would fill that emptiness that she had in her life.

While Don Greg was very cautious and a good provider for his daughters, they were not very happy with the comfort provided by his father. Therefore when the time came they began to escape one by one. The Villa of Don Greg, was surrounded by a high fence, apart from safeguarding the property, also avoided that his daughters would jump out of it without his permission. But once "love" struck and disturbed them, it didn't matter the height of the fence! Since they would jump it fleeing with whom would be their new "Owner." To give birth to children, and serve their husband was what the new life held for them after jumping the fence.

Whenever one of the girls escaped Don Greg became stricter and the rules were even more unbreakable. Something that was not convenient to Doña Igna. Apart from swinging in her swing and make a few chores she got bored as a "clam" and the only thing that mattered to her was to think that one day a -Prince Charming- would rescue her from that confinement. And why not, it would take her to walk and dance. Her older sisters had also suffered the loss of their mother and apart from caring for each other also had trained Doña Igna basics she should know as a housewife. But their mistake according to Doña Igna, was that they had "jumped the fence" and fled with a lover, which had limited Igna the possibility of being able to see -at least from afar- a good suitor. So when she met Don Ira and he offered "the sky and the stars" she did not hesitate to accept the opportunity, and so -the dove- one fine day escaped from her nest (where she had at least a roof and good food) to an unknown world, but she had decided to take that chance.

With his gallantry and several letters of affection, Don Ira persuaded Doña Igna, and invited her to embark on a new adventure full of dreams and fantasies. To start a new life where she would be "Queen of the House" and then would no longer have to receive orders from Don Greg. But Ira never told her that he would be whom would be giving orders thereafter. He had also promised that he would take her out for parties and new see places, and they would occasionally go to dance. With all "good intentions," then they planned their getaway. And with the help of a couple of friends and a moonless night, Don Ira rescue the Princess from her "cloister." And so she escaped by jumping the fence to a new life.

The next morning from the "getaway", Doña Igna faced the harsh reality, though it was not yet the full reality. After a month of living together she learned what her destiny had reserved for her, instead of freedom, she will have "many children." And that poor and empty home had taken the place of her home where the cheese Wattles hung of the beam in the barn, where giant pots of honey were always full, where the canned fruit was never missing and not to mention the grains and the milk of goat and cow. The more Igna compared what she had taken for granted, the more overwhelming her situation seemed. And to make matters worse "she lost her menses", something that no one had informed her that would happen when someone join her body to "a man" according to her. What Don Ira had planned for her,-to make up- was a wedding though poor but at least that.

Another lovely surprise was that Don Ira had ordered his new wife that she had to –put away- all makeup, tight clothing, high heels, and she needed to kept her jewels out of his sight since he was not happy to see her in that environment with all those ornaments. To complete the scene, it was a custom that after –their fault- they had to apologize to the father of the bride... Doña Igna thought so at least it would have support if everything would not go well. So one day they armed themselves with bravery, and went to ask for forgiveness. The father of the bride would be seated at the back of the room, the couple would go on their knees to where he was, and if everything worked out they were not to return until he decided to do so. But if not, they would go back to try again, until everything would be resolved. By good luck, Don Greg forgave them but warned them that he better do not hear -cries in the future- complaints about their decision they had taken, so that was his blessing.

Months later, Doña Igna noticed that she had gained a lot weight and that her small waist had disappeared. Thus, she had to look for a justification for such change. When she consulted with the healer – curandera-, she told her she was pregnant and she would give birth to a baby. The healer observing the face of surprise of the expectant mother, explained with patience what would happen when a couple live together. The shock was greater when the pregnancy came to an end, since the new mother didn't know how the creature would come to the world. Doña Igna justified her ignorance saying that as she was "daughter of family" in those days the daughters of family were not supposed to know too much about those duties, nor had to ask anything about the intimacy of couples, so those who married were completely blind since the more "innocent" they were, the most desirable maidens became and therefore the husband would appreciate them and even more men would respect them.

THE DISAPPOINTMENT AS A LIFESTYLE

The following years took away Doña Igna dream of "freedom and happiness." Those were "big words" that would never be mentioned in the bosom of the family or by any chance. Years went by, eventually Igna lost hope of more "comfortable" and normal life's expectations. Her days were spent listening to songs that only fed the grief of her days, her smile disappeared as well as the idea of going out to dance or have fun. Her slender body was disfigured due to the forced labor and all those births, -that she had not even imagined she would have when she swung on that swing so bored-. In her new home she had to pick up her beautiful long hair in a "bun" so no one would appreciate it –per Ira request-. She had lost her teeth almost completely and her skin–she cared so much -smooth and healthy, was then dry and stained for the lack of healthy food and rest.

Finally Igna had realized that her father was right when he warned that if she married a poor peasant without education, vocation, trade or purpose, her life would be a real torture (suffering). But she wanted to believe in the promise of Don Ira. Conversely, reality struck on her face, although she refused to believe it and accepted it. While her quality of life at her father's home had been better, covering the basic needs of food, shelter and dress. In her husband's house, she had to barely survive day by day as "doing magic" for will power. Igna had to stretch everything to be able to manage the little income that Don Ira brought her home. Her only hope was that one day her beloved sons would grow up and eventually they would compensate her all her great effort and sacrifice of life. Don Ira on the other hand, had forgotten the promises he had made to Doña Igna. On the contrary, he had concentrated on his "needs and responsibilities." Thereby he worked from sunrise to sunset in time of sowing season and when there was no much to do, he would order Igna to "prepare" his best clothing since he would go out to "distract himself" on weekends or "dominguear" as he said. While the poor lady stayed at home to meet her "obligations" as a homemaker, which represented a total insult to Igna who felt like a –total fool- to believe that that man would take her out with him. The other days of the week don Ira arrived tired from the "Milpa" and with bad mood, hitting all the children if approached him for any silly reason. The couple was just glad and a bit content when the children were babies and did not annoyed them so much. Doña Igna loved them only for a few moments when she thought that someday they would compensate all "the sacrifices." Thus, the couple were almost always tired and cranky since life was "cruel" and unfair to them.

Apart from the fact that Igna had to become a woman that would cover his "basic needs" Don Ira had in his mind that because "God had removed his brothers from earth" then it was responsibility of Doña Igna to "recover them" by giving him all the boys she could engender... Big compromise and responsibility was expected from Lady Igna, first serve and please her husband and then give him a lot of little kids to fill the "emptiness" that his deceased brothers had left. Neither had an idea that children who they were giving birth had their own needs and that it was not so easy to satisfy them especially if they lived in extreme poverty. While Don Ira presumed his wife to the rest of the peasants, telling them that he deserved a young and fertile woman who gave him good and healthy children; meanwhile Doña Igna was swallowing the frustrations and the desire to tell that what appeared to be a "happy family" it was only appearances.

Don Ira expected children to grow big, strong and hard workers, because he also needed to recover his "investment" of great effort from giving them deprivations of a poor roof and a poor meal. He said "no matter that today I work much, when they grow up they are going to pay with large bale of money." But it never occur to him, to think that in his dreams of "Alchemist" those little ones would need good nutrition and education to be able to compensate somewhat for his "investment." Don Ira always thought that education was for "lazy" people and they only had to "educate their children by example." According to Don Ira would be enough for the children to learn if alone the five vowels and numbers from one to 10 and sign their name. The rest would come "by osmosis."

As for food, he thought that they were not only live to eat, because the children were not "pigs of fattening" to later kill them an eat them. On the contrary, they had to eat very little to be light and fast to work. But Don Ira was the first who sat at the table and did not stop until it will fill up his stomach. He said that he had to eat well because he was who worked hard to "support" or bring -sustenance- to the House. While he was served with a bowl of stew with meat and sometimes ask for seconds, the children deserve only broth with bits of tortilla, while he drank a cup of boiled milk, the children drank a cup of tea with a spout of milk. So to the malnourished kids always took longer time to work move fast, and comply with their chores, but the order/rule was the same "that who does not work, do not eat," said Don Ira.

IN SEARCH OF A BETTER LIFE

The long awaited day had arrived to search for a better life style, that day that seemed like it would never become to present with its troubles and rush. Don Ira had finally realized that it was time to get out of the "quagmire" at that Ranch which had no more than sadness and laments. By that time some relatives had come from the big city trying to convince Ira that if he migrate to the city at list the children would have a bit better life. After thinking over and over again about the possibilities, he decided to give it a try. First he went "solo" and got a job in a factory. After a month or so, he saved some money and came back to the ranch to pick up the starving family… Thus, one fine day the family packed up their tiliches (belongings) and prepared for the new journey. The next day very early all arose. With tight stomach and the vague hope of a better life in an unknown world and far away from home. Once everyone got on the bus, no one wanted to even look to what was left behind. Perhaps because of the fear of thinking that if they did, their departure would be more painful. Thus began the journey that would last for at least 12 hours.

Arriving to the city, with so much noise from the traffic and people, the poor family was so stunned and exhausted, they did not even ask or expressed anything. All piled up and starving it appeared that they had been removed from a concentration camp. Contrary to what Ana was expecting to see, she found a smaller space than what they had in the ranch and more crowded than what she was used to see. A nephew of Don Ira had made him the great favor of renting him "two rooms." A room would be used as a bedroom, and the other would be the kitchen and dining room. Ana thought for a moment, "well probably only be temporary" things would improve soon. That was her wishful thinking.

As always happens where there were many people and many children, the problems began to emerge, the kids were trying to adapt to their new environment and it was hard for them to get used to a new and limited space, without patio to play or a place to go out to run. It was very chaotic situation. They fought with the other children from the other half of the house and the adults did not know how to resolve the conflict rationally. And to make matters worse, only three months after having arrived to the city, Don Ira and Doña Igna decided to continue what already was usual for them "to make more children." So there she was again pregnant! There was no awareness and -they seemed to be clueless- that all of the children slept on the floor made of cement, that there was only a wage of worker barely reaching for the most deficient needs. Without even knowing if there would be enough food for another day, not to mention take a glass of milk or juice calmly. The crisis continued!

After, long conversation without reaching major ends, Don Ira e Igna decided it was time to look for another place close by to take their big family and another in the way and having a separate place to live. There was then another home but similar to the one they were living in; now the family had to share the living space with a strange family who used the wall as a division of both residences, and again was only 2 rooms one for the family to sleep and other to cook and eat. And since there were no enough space to sleep in the cold and hard floor in the main room, some kids had to sleep in the kitchen corner. But no one had to complaint about it since family had to be thankful than they were not homeless. But the parents continued reproducing more babies like there was no other things to do.

FROM THE SMALL TO
THE BIG JUNGLE

It came the time to send the children to school and the complaints were up in the environment. As Don Ira had to buy school supplies to the kids and the uniform which was mandatory. Where in the world he would get money for such things as "rare" in the city? But life had to continue, like if that was not a problem. Reluctantly and with "much sacrifice" Don Ira was able to buy the uniforms to the kids, but they better do not ask him for nothing more. Since nothing more would be available, there would be no money for lunch or snacks at school, the kids had to conform to a cup of tea and animal cookies as breakfast and to wait until they got home to see if there was something more nutritious when they would come back from school.

The first day of classes was a real adventure, Ana and her siblings had to find a place among dozens of students at the school. She and her brothers had never seen so much kids at the same time. The ranks were endless. Ana thought, "Where so many people come from?" Was a real conundrum finding her place in the long line. The teacher with a face of "disgust" told her to take any place that it was in the first row since Ana did not grow due to malnutrition, although it was one of the oldest in age she had to fit with the shortest children in the row who were a year or two younger than her.

Apart from having to cope with teasing from the other students that obviously noticed the lack of socialization of Ana and her clothes "second hand." Ana also had to learn to speak without an accent and with the "lingo" of the "city." Also had to deal with a teacher who had a very bad temper "like a thousand demanding demons." Who was easily bothered by everything from the appearance of the students to their "slow" learning skills. Ana had realized that the only way to avoid problems was to try to make everything more acceptable and stay quiet most of the time. Although Ana had good memory and tried to learn as much as possible, yet was not missing from the scolding of the teacher by the slightest thing.

On one occasion, the teacher asked all students to do a summary of the history of "Helen Keller." The requirements were that they had to put the date in the upper right side of the sheet, save the corresponding margins, and sign the summary at the bottom right of the page. With the nerves of the penetrating gaze of the teacher at least one of the requirements of the writing had been forgotten by most of the students. So the teacher did not hesitate to punish them all. He formed them outside of the classroom to give them shame, one by one, hit them in the hands with a yardstick and not mattered if it hurt or not, the teacher only insulted them whenever he beat them with it.

There were other students who irritated the teacher, sometimes he threw them the blackboard eraser, other went and pulled them from their seat, passing them to the front and made them count the times he would pull of their hair, and didn't care if it was a girl or a boy anyway he called them "idiots." The strongest punishment was when on one occasion he had pulled the hair of a student, and got a louse in his hand. The teacher then asked all students to step outside from the classroom and check them with two pencils, then he ordered to cut their hair totally out of the head. And the girls cropped hair and none children would show up to resume class if they would not comply with his orders.

So the next day, everyone returned to class with the shaved head and girls with very short hair. The teacher saw them and made fun of all. But the punishment seemed very cruel to Ana. So tired of the abuse that she saw and armed with unusual bravery she found a way to ask for a hearing with the principal. By good luck that the principal did not refuse to receive her. Ana explained with much fear and detail what was going on in that classroom. She was taking the risk that if the abusive teacher discovered her feat would expel her from the class. Ana ensured that it was Friday so he would forget what had happened if the principal would bring the issue to his attention.

No one mentioned anything next week. Ana tried to hide the guilt of her feat. But apparently the teacher did not discover it or if he did, probably would have been warned to not mistreat more students. Apart there was something different, another teacher was present in the class. So probably that was the reason why there was no riot. A week later the nag teacher did not show up for class, and everyone wondered what would have happened. The time of the Christmas break was approaching and that would help things to get sorted out or at least they cool down according to Ana.

When they returned to class after the Christmas and New Year break, all the children noticed a calmer atmosphere, besides the group had a substitute teacher. Although some asked what would have happened with the cranky teacher, there was not a complete answer. Almost at the end of the school year, the grouchy teacher returned, but apart from the fact that his head was shaved, his facial expression was also quite different. His attitude was better than the one before, after observing the face of interrogation of students, he explained in a very simple way that the surgeon had taken a piece of brain that had cut from the "corpus collosum" that unites the two hemispheres of the brain and which had help him to smooth his temper. For all students the news sounded like a glass of cool water in summer. So it was the end of the school year. Ana felt very satisfied and relieved, because apart from having managed to be among the top five students with highest scores, it had also managed to calm down the teacher.

THE LARGE FAMILY LIVES WORST

Meanwhile at Ana's home the crisis continued, due to the birth of the youngest of the family, Don Ira had decided to find another place to live. As he could not find or pay something bigger or better, he got half of another house with the same dimension, two bedrooms. In the single room Don Ira and Doña Igna put their bed and barely had room for the rest of the family who would be sleeping on the floor. But there was not enough room for Ana, so she had to sleep in a corner of the kitchen on the floor colder and harder than an iceberg. But that was not important, while proliferation was at its peak.

The birth of the new member of the family was quite an event, only for Don Ira and Doña Igna, the rest of the family was not so happy seeing the situation in which they lived. For this reason, the doctor had advised Igna to stop calving. Not only her body was completely worn out by the usage, the poor Lady had already lost all her teeth, the doctor also had told her that she had to lose her hair —cut it off- since it was all thin and apparently was draining her calcium as having children was doing. The doctor could not imagine how the whole family lived, if so he could have suffered the swoon. So the Lady had argued with the doctor about his intrusion; but because of the resistance of Doña Igna, the doctor had devised a plan.

When the Lady would be sedated by the anesthesia during the delivery of the baby in the hospital, the doctors would take her to the operating table and would tie her tubes so she would stop given birth to more children given the poverty and deprivation the rest of the children lived in. They did not consider the cunning of the lady, who after given birth to a lot of kids, she did not even fell asleep after childbirth. When she gave birth to the little one, the nurses thought she was asleep, so they drove her to the operating room, but she was not completely asleep so without measuring any risk, she jumped off from the table and rushed herself out of it insulting everyone.

Lady Igna was discharged from the maternity room–given the circumstances- so she came home with the new offspring. To make the situation worst, the people who came to visit her kept saying that the "Cherub" was "so beautiful" that she should not "stop calving." Nobody was thinking about the rest of the family wellbeing… Igna could not even attend Ana's elementary school graduation since she was convalescent and according to her, she couldn't carry the baby to such an event. Her concentration at that time was to see the little one who she had given birth, even though it would give her a headache to think that the baby would eat every day. So for comfort she was playing with the Cherubim and she even took a lot of pictures of him to do portraits and placed them in the home like a Gallery, in the single room where all other children slept, as showing them that only one who matter was the Cherub.

Don Ira, on the other hand, hated having to pay rent and in his mind was always the idea of building his own "home." So after giving many turns to the topic of child birth control, he decided to agree on sending Doña Igna to be tied to "stop calving". So as if it were the great sacrifice, Lady Igna accepted but also had an episode of depression. She did not want to know anything about anyone else. Ana and other family members were responsible for caring for the family while Igna recovered from the depression. As there was not much to eat, Ana went to seek for work at her 12 years of age to see who would employ her at least to help with the household chores. Ana was not even thinking about the shame of cleaning or helping with household chores, she only cared to eat something better than what she was given at home. Apart from going to school, Ana had to take care of her siblings and help with chores, also made enough time to go visit the "rich" houses and see if she could help to run some errands or personal things or at least to do dishes in order to get some little money.

At that time the Government had implemented a campaign of urbanization, and had decided to sell the federal lands that were in the foothills of the sierras. So only the "poorest" could buy those lands since it would take them much time to install them water and drainage or electricity services. Don Ira was touched by luck so he grabbed a small piece of land in that place. With great sacrifice, he built two rooms of-block of cement with a roof of galvanized sheet metal. Finally the big family had their "humble home". They did not know what kind of people would live in the new colony. Apart from extreme poverty there were families who had as many as 20 kids also all malnourished and uneducated living in ticuruches (shacks) of cardboard sheets that they called home. Beside the family of Don Ira, lived a family of an old lady with a couple of adult children, ugly and smelly. Then in the next "home" lived a prostitute who fought all the time with clients and had deformed children. When Ana contemplated that rotten world of people could not avoid claim to Don Ira why he had chosen such a depressing place to live. Don Ira replied that was all that he could provide to his family and if it that was not enough or if Ana was not satisfied with it, then she and the rest of children had to start working to buy something better.

Don Ira started sending the children -who were poorly dressed and malnourished- to 'shine shoes and sell lemons at the market. One of the kids used to sing songs to see if people would give a little money for his talent. Apart from the fact that they gave him some pennies for candy, one lucky day the Director of the kinder garden heard him singing and caused her sympathy. So she gave him a scholarship for kinder garden registration for one year. He was the only one in the family who was able to attend the kinder garden and therefore was able to continue school with very good grades. He continued elementary school with excellent grades and won the privilege to travel to important points in the Mexican Republic. Only then the parents of the little brown "morenito" were proud of him.

FROM GUATE-MALA TO GUATE-WORSE

Living without drinking water, having no bathroom, tissue paper or the basics was the only thing Ana could see, and just trying to survive and do not commit any atrocity, the best thing to do was to continue going to school for as long as she could, thought Ana. Between blows, scolding and insults, Ana lived thinking that the school would be the only escape. So against "wind and tide" she managed to continue attending school and helping with the chores at home. In the morning she helped to clean the house, wash dishes and babysitting, as well as bring the water from the "pipe" if it did not reach that street that day. Sometimes she did not have time to eat, and would not eat at school either, so she was almost asleep —sometimes- due to the hunger and fatigue. During class she was doing her assignments, but even so sleepy, she knew to correctly answer the questions of the teacher. Ana had to do homework in the evening since she didn't have time during the day. But even so her scores were always the best not only of the classroom but also at home.

Ana enrolled herself in high school as her parents did not cared much about it. As she had very good grades, no one put obstacles to accept the registration. Ana had decided that the only way to find a better job in the future should be education. Therefore she tried hard to get the best grades. Her efforts bore fruit when she graduated from the first year of high school, then she occupied the second place of all the group of 45 students. Dalia was the first but her parents owned a grocery store so, again the food helped her a little to her intellect. Ana thought to herself, "Sometimes the lectures do not enter when someone is hungry" and imagined how it would have been her life if at least she could eat meat, milk and fruit every other day.

When Ana entered a second year of high school, she faced another challenge. The teacher in charge of the group was very aggressive. She always dressed in tight denim pants and had a pretty stocky body that if someone saw it from the back would think she was a strong man. To complete the scene she used the hair very short and hated the makeup, so her presence more than inspiring respect, intimidated students. She said that she was an attorney but she was bored of her practice and therefore it was better for her to teach history and civics classes. So instead of administrating routine exams every other month, she gave them each month. When applied the first test to the group, she nearly failed all. Those who had the highest ratings in first year of high school were the only ones who passed with a score of "8" which was not acceptable per Ana's expectations.

When Ana saw her score, she felt very disappointed and made her sick to her stomach. How was that possible that someone who did not know her well could insult her by giving an "8" when she was used to have only "10"? She then decided to confront the teacher. All the rest of students remained quiet when they saw Ana approaching the teacher with a face of disgust. When she asked for a logical explanation to the score, the teacher became enraged, and said: "so you think you very smart ass" and asked Ana to recite the "29 individual guarantees of the Mexican Constitution" then she will see if she deserved a higher rate. Ana asked then a time to memorize them and the teacher gave her a week. The following week the students were on the lookout for the challenge. When the time came, the teacher asked Ana to stand in front of the classroom and recite the "29 individual guarantees of the Constitution." Ana felt her legs trembled, but she did it. Everyone hoped that Ana collapsed under the pressure, but Ana did not stop not for a second, until she finished reciting them all without interruption. All were astonished and speechless, even the teacher seemed impressed.

But still the teacher was not satisfied with Ana's affront, then asked Ana that next week she needed to learn all the most important countries of the world map with all their respective capitals. But as she suspected that Ana would not accept the challenge without questioning then this time made all students to learn at least the countries of each continent separately, so she assigned a continent to a certain small group of students and other continent to a different group so they could not escape her mandate. Everyone hated Ana, since by her boldness the entire group had to exercise the brain more. And as apparently that hurts, and they had to blame someone for their pain. The following week, the teacher did not asked Ana to make the recitation, instead made a more comprehensive review to it and left the rest of the students had other shorter test. At the time of giving the results the teacher was surprised again. Ana had scored 95% correct in the exam, while others barely reached the passing score and others not even got 50%. Was then when the teacher did not challenge Ana again and when the year was over told her, "You have a good future do not surrender."

When Anna graduated from high school, her mother could not attend since she had no time for "nonsense events." Therefore Ana's father sympathized with her and sat among the audience of parents who were interested in their children graduation from high school. The school had assigned as master of ceremony the teacher who had given headaches to Ana, when it was the turn of Ana to receive her diploma, the teacher shook her hand and said "congratulations you will achieve something someday..." Later she approached Ana's father and said "I congratulate you, you have a daughter with lots of character, and she is going to be someone in the future. " To which the father of Ana replied "well of course yes, the sons of Don Ira are none damn" the teacher drew a smile of acceptance and told Ana "now I know where the character is coming from," and wish good luck.

Finally Ana completed high school. But with the high school alone she could not find work unless she work as a maid or factory worker. So Ana did attempt to get a job in a factory, even though in her mind was always the idea of working for a while until she saved a bit of money to enter college. She worked during 2 or 3 months; so she was able to buy her first new pants and first bed since she was tired of sleeping on the floor. The job didn't last long and Ana continued looking for work in shops and small businesses without finding something that would satisfy her, or at least that could save some money for the future. Due to the extreme poverty in which she lived, Ana did not dare to dream like any other teen, while the girls were crazy about boys and dreamed of growing older and see how they made "perfect couples", Ana just thought in grow and learn as much as possible, and be able to find the solution to the poverty and ignorance that surrounded her and smothered her every day.

EDUCATING THE FAMILY

Between her own struggle for survival and her parents' complaints, Ana was trying to make some peace out of that chaotic situation. She thought that was her responsibility to help the family by telling them "what life was about." At the age of 12 y/o Ana observed how the family lived day by day in a routine they were immerse living without think on a different life style. At the time there were 8 children at home and one in the way about to be born. Ana tried to make some sense from that scenario asking her mother why do they had to live like that. Why not thinking on a better life. Her mother only repeated the same response, "You know nothing about life...I do not know why you complaint so much." Ana was only trying to make sense out of their way of thinking.

Surrounded by indigents, delinquents and prostitutes, it was very difficult if not impossible to make a change and to prevent her brothers to become part of that putrid community. Although most of the family members had activities to do during the weekend. Ana decided to interrupt them to give them the "speech of the week" either on Saturday morning or Sunday morning. In the weekend the boys woke up late and they usually turned on the music and the TV to watch the soccer game. It seemed like a "mad house." Even when they had "activities" most of the time was spent making noise at home. Ana was tired of picking up their mess since they did not even pick up their dirty socks and left the all over the room. But one day she did not ask them anymore to turn down the radio or TV. She just did it herself. After turning off all the noise, Ana ordered them to go to the porch and sit around the table.

Then Ana started her "speech" and said "Life is not about working and barely making it like a non- rational animal, life is about making yourself better of how you came to this world… this is not life, just living a messy life in a miserable place. You need to think about the future and how your life will be in 5 or 10 years… You have to stop making excuses, you need to be the best in school, and at any activity you do, starting by picking up after yourselves at home." Most of the boys walked away muttering about what Ana was saying. They commented that all of the "speech" as not more than "tacos de lengua" aka non-sense talking. Ana did not discouraged and continue every week trying to educate the family. In one occasion the father join them, and after listening to Ana's talk, he said "Poor Ana she does not know what life is about, just let her talk, one day when she find a man he will straight her up…"

Ana insisted in her journey of awakening her brothers out of that "poor thinking," she continued giving them the "speech" everything she could hold them to listen to her. Years went by, and Ana would continue saying " you need to think about the future, what kind of lives you are going to live, are you going to progress and live a better life? Or just living poor and ignorant for the rest of your lives? Ana's brothers, just answered, "You are crazy thinking life could be any different of what we are living in right now. You are dreaming that people like us can be different than the way we were born, you need to wake up! Look around you, there is nothing of what you telling us, we live in an extreme poverty because that is our destiny, we are humble and poor and that is the way we have to live life…" Ana was getting more and more stressed out since she could not show them an example of "real people" who had overcome such misery. Other than those in the books.

In spite of all the resistance, Ana started to show them how to wash their socks and underwear by hand since sometimes the old washing machine was broken. Ana also show them how to make quick meals and to wash the dishes. Her mother was always against her saying Ana would make them "gays" and it would be her fault that they would not turn into "real men." Ana's father was also very upset about the issue, "I can wait to see how a man is going to make her stop such craziness and put her in her place," for what Ana answered, " Yes when you find that person, bring it over to me and will teach him how to be a "man." Ana decided to stop her speeches and just teach by example. About half of her brothers learned how to pick up after themselves and make a quick meal. Regardless of her parents scolding and fears. One of her younger brothers whom Ana not even taught how to be self-sufficient, started his own journey and learned how to cook so well that even his mother was surprised about his "culinary skills." However, his father was not so happy since later in his life he went to live with another gay and they lived "happy ever after." That was a real shocking news to his father who thought that his boy will be just like him "macho men and proliferating." The rest of those who followed Ana's directives eventually got married and have good wives and steady families. While the others were almost there but thinking what have they "done wrong" and how they could not to be like the ones who have a better lifestyle.

THE IDEAL FIGURE

Ana was 15 years old, and any girl in that age only cared about how they looked and measured their waist trying to match the "ideal figure." Others were preparing for the "Quinceañera" party. The parents of Ana did not even deigned to acknowledged her or ask how she like a gift for reaching the 15 as other parents used to do. Nobody even mentioned the birthday of Ana or the faintest intention of having a party "Quinceanera." Ana's mother instead of sympathizing or nurturing her self-esteem, showed her a dress that – she had saved from when she was 15 years old-. Just to rub it in her face "I had a body by the age of 15". Never occurred to her to think for a moment that she had lived a totally different life. That life without limitations of food or that she (Igna) had appropriate and balanced meals; while the poor Ana had to eat what was left after everyone else ate. And therefore she not yet developed body of woman due to malnutrition. When Igna asked Ana to try the "stupid dress," Lady Igna drew a mocking smile when she saw 'that damn dress" had not entered Ana's body who "without female figure" tried it... Igna had hurt her feelings again. But the young Ana did not dismay instead it started another challenge: she would have to demonstrate to Igna that one can transforms the body easily, but the mind of some people would take much longer.

To complete the scene, Igna spread the comments that all "young ladies" shall be pretty according to- Doña Igna-. Apart from continuously make comments about the body development of her nieces, Igna also attempted to hurt Ana's pride to see how she reacted when commented about some "handsome guys." Anything that resembled a "man" would be good for her favorite daughter according to her. As Ana already knew what the intention of the Lady was, she answered her that if she (Igna) wanted them she could keep them, since Ana was not ready to let the hormone rule like everyone else was. By then -outraged Igna- insulted her saying that probably Ana was not enough female (straight) and that maybe Ana was a "lesbian." She also said that there was something wrong with her because all the other girls were crazy about guys and she was not, thus she was a 'a piece of work"... For years Ana's mother said the same things mean comments to Ana, "women have to take care of themselves and be very nice to be able to deserve the affection of a man or a husband" said Igna. She had not a clue that Ana was constantly besieged by the men when she was out in the streets.

To prove Doña Igna wrong, Ana got a job at a gym. The schedule was long, from 7:00 o'clock in the morning to 10:00 in the evening. But she had 3 hours of break at noon. During those three hours, Ana took advantage to take classes of aerobics and weights. In less than 4 months Ana managed to develop a fit /good body. As she ate healthier food from the nutrition bar of the gym. With the exhaustive exercise the stomach fat disappear and she developed her bust and buttocks. Once Ana figure out that she had lost weight, asked Igna for the dress she bragged about, and tried again this time it fit, but it was tight in the bust since Ana had developed a near-perfect bust which her mother did not have when she was a young girl. Then her mother said to her "that is all artificial, and it is not something natural" –men will look at you from far-, but when they look closer, they will not see your "natural beauty..." Ana had realized by then, that she would never please Igna. Instead of insisting on proving her point to Igna, Ana decided to continue educating herself looking for better things to do... Ana could not fit well with her cousins because she was not thinking on mating or vanities. Due to her rebellious and revolutionary ideas, Ana got rejected from the "Club of Beauties", but Ana did not care about it, because she had faith that one day she would demonstrate also to them that there are more important things in life than the nonsense of youth.

THE CLAN OF BEAUTIES

Another of the novelties observed by Ana was that the vast majority of families had moved to the city also. But for them the situation was different. For instance, her cousins had found a way to not only adapt to the new life, but to "ignore" the shortcomings which the rest of the family passed through. They had their own way of escape of reality. Thus, they formed the "Clan of the Beauties" since, everything would stay in the "family." All of them gathered at home of the oldest cousin to talk about their adventures, failures and other things. They also drank and danced, while others would go distracted "despistadas" to practice another type of "forbidden games" that later would show some consequences.

The Clan of beauties was formed by female cousins and male cousins (girls and boys), Pita was the oldest of all, and "they respected" her because she was not doing anything bad, she was only very hardworking and "very dedicated to the house." She was the daughter of Vito (the newspaper of the Ranch). Pita also helped her younger brothers who tried to improve themselves, -although not everything went as she thought-. She had also sacrificed her youth working, not allowed to have many boyfriends like the rest of the clan. Apart of that, she already passed the 30s still remained "Miss" (virgin) according to her. That was why she was considered a role model daughter and also an example to follow according to those who knew her. Therefore, most of the parents of the other cousins didn't make a fuss in the fact that they would meet in her house every weekend.

The younger brothers of Pita were: May, Hetor, and Mary. May and Hetor, were meant to be teachers according to the plans of Pita, but "IQ" did not help them much because they had not much in their "Knucklehead" as a result they could not pass the school year. Although they tried several times, they were no able to graduate from "teaching" and ended up working in a local factory. Mary which had never been the brightest in the class, and instead of developing intellect, developed figure, -according to her other cousins-, was trying "the career" of Commercial Secretary. But she and Pita thought that she only needed a tall and slender figure and long abundant hair, in order to be "Secretaria." Mary was in the shorthand and typing classes, when she realized that intelligence and motor skills were also needed. So as much as she tried to pass these two classes, she could not do it, because she could never type quickly enough and although she was attractive she could not graduate from Commercial Secretary.

After the resounding failure of attempts to educate herself, the beautiful Mary had not many choices, the only option left was to use her "beauty." Thus, for the sexy girl (Mary), the choice was to conquer a good man who at least deigned to marry her. So, showing off her long hair and slender figure she tried to conquer the son of the corner's grocery store. Who was a pretentious young guy who pretended to have "a lot of money" Mary was not using much of her brain, she thought that if she gave the guy what he asked (the taste of love) he would feel compelled to compromise and it would "hook" him for a quick marriage. Big mistake! The guy took what was offered or given to him and as "Pontius Pilate, washed his hands." Suddenly the "brunette" began to feel ill, and as the month went by, she noticed a delay on her menses. When Mary told the guy about the "good news," he acted like nothing had happened and ended the relationship. As a result, the only option left was to look for the "family support." Mary's family noticed that there was "something wrong" since her behavior and physical appearance was not the same. After trying several ways of find out what was going on. They concluded that "the girl was pregnant."

Pita did not know where to hide the head for the "shame" and she could not believe who was the one responsible for "the favor," since the "girl" told the family that the guy was not responsible for any damage incurred. They concluded then, that they had to find a solution to the problem. In those days, "abortion" was not very common and doctors were unleashing to provoke it. Since that was the only alternative, to "get rid of the package" Mary's mother and Pita found a "witch woman" who would help her get rid of 'the problem." A few days later, Mary was seen again with her skinny figure and a face of "repentance" only she could carried it. A few days passed and she recovered a little of her "wrongdoing" and had learned that "playing with fire" was not the best solution. Then decided to find a job as Secretary, although she had not completed the education as such, she hoped to get a job in an office. But the luck was not very good with her, and had to accept a job as a factory worker in the local factory.

After so many ravages the beauty of Mary had not disappeared yet, she still retained her slim figure and long and well-groomed hair. While at work in the factory there were men and women so, the men could not miss to put their eyes on her. The man who fell in love with her was so impressed with her "beauty" that decided to ask for marriage. When Mary told her family about the "good intentions" of the man, her mother and Pita decided to be "honest" with the future groom, and when he went to "ask for her hand" (for marriage), they told him about the "mistake (misstep)" done previously by the "girl." Thinking that the man would accept her and forgave her anyway. But although he was a poor and uneducated man, he claimed its "dignity" and felt betrayed saying he had been duped by Mary's beauty, because she had not told him of her "failure/fiasco" from the beginning of their courtship. It was in this way that Mary "bait business" and as a result, she could not get a decent wedding.

Given the circumstances of the event, all the decent wedding plans had vanished. Revealed the "secret," promises and dreams vanished. But although the man was disappointed, he still "in love" and he continued seeing Mary, -until a not too distant day-, he decided to convince her that he would forgive "her sin" only if she wanted to continue the relationship under his terms. Then the man suggested a deal, although it wasn't the most splendid, at least would redeem her from her "fault" since otherwise nobody "would accept her". As the self-esteem of poor Mary was already on the ground, she was left with no other option, than to accept its proposal to go live with him even without any promise of marriage. So it was then that one fine day Mary left to live with the man who extended his hand to amend her "mistakes." The first thing he did apart from take her to live in a place poor and gross (dirty), he had no compassion for Mary and bought her a "hot dogs" cart and put her to sell them at the bus stop. Then he got her pregnant with a couple of little kids. And so it was how it turned the life of one "beauty" of the clan.

The other group of cousins were, Malen, Marty, Rodo, Soco and Rule. They were the children of aunt Guani and all were elementary school teachers, or at least trying to be. Malen had been the first to graduate from teaching, and had encouraged her brothers to achieve the same career. She was the second in command of the clan, but as physiological needs do not forgive the human body, she suddenly slipped out of meetings of the Saturday night and started "playing the games that people play." So they soon had its result and to amend it, she planned a quick wedding thus nobody suspected of her "little mistake." Marty the next in the string of "teachers", also tried her own adventures, and when she decided to introduce her suitor to her parents, the suitor who she had chosen, was not of their approval. But since she was already "independent" and her will was stronger due to the "evidence" which was about to get noticed, she also undertook the flight with her lover and eventually married so it was born the "surfeit" of nine months. Rodo on the other hand, was very "shy" even though he had succeeded in his studies of teaching, he was not very attractive and stuttered; so although he gather together with "the group" its complex burned his insides since it was not easy to find a partner outside the circle of "cousins." For good or bad luck, there was another cousin with the same complex of "inferiority" since she had a problem in her eye which was "going sideways," when the two disgraceful souls found each other, the arrow of Cupid was not made to wait, and though the world was opposed to their relationship as cousins "in first grade" they didn't care about others; thus they joined their sorrows and their bodies and were exiled from the clan. The youngest of the string, Soco and Rule they were also unappealing, just enjoyed the "chatter" with the rest of the cousins and behave well due to their age and lack of appeal.

The following female cousin was the "Cute" since life was not very splendid as to provide her with a sexy figure or any grace, also had its small problem of "inferiority." Since childhood had made her derision because she had a "bad" eye, apparently the mother had taken the poor baby out in the cold when she had "fever" one eye had move to the side and never came back to its normality. Apart from poverty in which she lived, Cute could not educate herself. So she had several reasons to think that she deserved not much, according to the parameters of the clan. Therefore it was difficult to get a boyfriend. Thus it was Rodo "first cousin" who made her "the favor" and eventually, the two fled to make a "different" life outside the family circle, who condemning them for their "sin" and "sacrilege." Someone commented that after the banishment, they had consummated their love and produced "normal children" since everyone expected to come out "Down" due to the "crossing blood" of the family.

Grace was another beauty of the clan, she believed she was the artist "Raquel Walsh" at least that was what the clan believed. Daughter of the teacher who had tried to "take advantage' from the aunt Mar. From her birth her destiny had been marked by "prematurity." Since the teacher -Grace's father- of the ranch had tried to take advantage (got pregnant out of wedlock) of aunt Mar. But Uncle Travis had threat the teacher if he would not amended his fault, and as a result was forced to marry her. So although very pretty the creature, had its small mark of "birth". Grace had also studied and graduated as teacher, so she was ahead of the game, by being educated and also beautiful. Apart from be or feel "pretty", not a silly, following the father steps who was also a school teacher and considered a very respectful person. Therefore she was given the luxury of taking or leaving with whom she picked and chosen, and changed boyfriends as one change her underpants. But instinct is sometimes stronger than the intelligence, suddenly she lost the "moon" her menses, and she was feeling in unusual way. By living life so fast (la Vida loca), it wasn't novelty that she could get pregnant. And to "cover the Sun with a finger," Grace had to marry soon to give a home to the result of its deployment of sexuality. But since Grace still attractive after childbirth, she fell in love with another bystander of a motorcycle. And she pick up and left with him to live the adventure, leaving the shoot with the father.

The next beauty was the "blonde" (Guera) who had ravings of artist. It changed name in the same way she changed underwear "chones." Sometimes she called herself Johana, others Roxana, others believed she was "Farrah Faucet" and "Sandy" of (Vaseline), suddenly she appeared as Yuri (the singer). As she didn't have very good self-esteem, she thought that men soured flowers (compliments), but all were obscenities "leperadas" that were saying on the street as if they were a very nice compliment. She worked as maid in a wealthy community- the Colonia Del Valle-. She said that she dressed as a bimbo "riquilla" since it wore the clothes that the daughters of her employer left to use whenever they bought new clothes. La Guera did not accept to be only the maid of wealthy houses, she wanted to be the owner of one of them. She said that if she dressed well maybe could hook up with a wealthy man and she could conquer a "junior" from the Valle's community. Therefore she decided to use most of her salary in transforming her image of "Cinderella" into "Sandy." In such a way that she bought satin pants, pearl color and one black well tight to the body. She thought that those were pants everyday use. But actually those pants were only used to dance in the "disco." So when she wore them on the street the jerks shout her obscenities –leperadas- but since she did not receive many positive compliments, she accepted those swear words. Because of her delusions of grandeur the blonde (Guera) did not realize that the "Sandy" was Nordic, high, thin, blue-eyed blonde and she used those pants just for the movie.

As the blonde (Guera) had observed that dress up "provocative" did not give her more than the "wrong idea" to the guys in the street, she decided to deploy its "beauty" in the "disco" where she danced as "parrot on a hot griddle" in those times of "mania" she met her "John"-thinking she was "Sandy"- she called him her "friend of dance" but John had another friend, both with the same "problem of identity" they believed to be "Stasky and Hutch". Therefore the situation was complicated, since she thought that she had met with "John" of "Vaseline" but they felt they were not dancers but actors. Between "pears or apples" the blonde felt like a "million bucks" with her two "friends." On one occasion she came up with the idea of inviting them to her "humble home" and for her bad luck, her father was there. When la Guera presented her "friends" to her father his face almost fell of shame, " hey little girl, men are not friends of women." The father of Guera could not make any sense of it. To which she replied, "don't be so outdated this is the fashion now." Her father said" When will my crazy girl get sane?" But that concept was perpetuated and later the father said "It appears like she will never compose herself."

Continuing with her delusion that she was "very beautiful" for being "Guera" she worked on getting a certificate on "typing" because she thought it was very sexy it would not be hard to get a good job, as a secretary. So she began her career of Secretaria. If before she believed she was "divine crane" after more she had risen "category" then was no longer the "divine crane" had become "a royal eagle" according to her perception. Therefore she was buying brand perfumes and arranging her hair with "lights" and fine makeup. She thought she will conquer an "Executive" and humiliated all men who approach her who did not have a thing to offer. After a while she convinced herself that "Prince charming" will not appear soon. Because what the chiefs offered were "indecent proposals", and the suitor she was looking for was not among them. It was then when she decided to continue her preparatory studies. And she enrolled in the night school for workers. She wanted to study to become an "Attorney" after graduating from preparatory school and to enroll in "the Faculty of Law." But the "blonde" was having a hard time to find her "Prince Charming" so instead she found her "little giant."

The blonde (Guera) thought that she was the only one in the night school that could draw attention, but soon realized that there were others like her. She wore her Secretary's uniform to impress teachers and dreamed of hooking one up. Thus, she would take pictures with them to see if they were also interested. In her "crazy mind" she imagined that those who did her the favor of photographing with her were in love with her; later would discover that everything they wanted was to have a little fun. When finally she "catch up" and realized the dimension of her delusion, she realized the true intentions of the "teachers." But as she was very "sociable" decided to put her eyes on one who was not on their level. He was among her "suitors" and quite different from them, but later would become the fortnight "owner," the "gallant Pepin" The poor guy didn't even had steady job. It was one of the oldest siblings of a family of twenty brothers. He had 19 brothers and they had several fathers (his mother liked the variety). When the Guera heard about his family situation (large and dysfunctional), she sympathized with him, according to her she would do him a favor "to improve the species." So the "little giant" as she called it–because it was her height,–conquered her eventually. Later the little giant (short) would lead her to the altar and then to "the dump" but that was only for a while until they got a decent place. Sometime later they could get their humble home, and it was as well as the "little giant" made her a chubby little girl –panzoncita- she looked exactly like him, not just on the physical but also intellectual mind. Yes, the Guera had improved her species.

The exclusive cousins were the Mayor's daughters. They were called the princesses. The oldest princess Feona barely talked since she was very shy. She was kind of distracted most of the time. She used to forget things when asked and sometimes she forgot where she was in "the world." On one occasion she forgot she was waiting for the bus at the bus's stop and started sucking her finger, people started laughing (since she was already a teenager), and she got so embarrassed... The younger, princess Diana was very aloof she did not want to mingle with the rest of the cousins because she was not of the same "social class." So there were the 2 princesses thinking they will grow up out of the misery and never would suffer like the rest of the "poor cousins." But one day the Mayor of the town –their father- decided to abandon the "perfect family" to go out and "enjoy life" with his secretary, who was 25 years younger than him. The whole family was devastated! How could something like that happen to them?

Since they thought they were the "untouchables" and very "exclusive" they had only few friends who could actually "stick" with the family. Thus, there were the 2 princesses and 2 other boys trying to overcome the "bad moment" of the family. The younger princess was going to the university at that time. She thought she was smarter than everyone else and was trying to become a lawyer. She concentrated on finishing college as soon as possible. Soon, she graduated from college and in the first opportunity she had, she "took off." No one knew why or how she found the man, who seemed to have money because later people muttered that she was a "missioner" along with the man. After a while some relatives said she got settled in a foreign country and had started a family.

Meanwhile the princess Feona, could not endure the betrayal of the Mayor and as soon as she could, got in touch with an alien man. No one knew how she could do that, since she barely finished high school. Regardless, of the opinion of the rest of the family she made the arrangements to marry that man and "flew" to the USA. People said she did that because she either was afraid of her parents' disapproval or she was already "knocked down." Later when she was formally married and had a couple of children, she presented the "Shrek" to the family. Apparently the reason of her "shame" was because he was about 20 years older than her and had already his own baggage... But after knowing the grandchildren the family had forgotten about the "issue." After that she started to "brag" about how "perfect" her family was, although her husband looked older than her father.

After observing the failure of the plan of the "clan" to keep the "family together," Pita the Director of the clan had giving up to what did not work, since they could not agree in their intentions and more, they would either were fighting or were pregnant. After such disappointment, Pita then decided to say "Yes" to an old boyfriend she had and put an end to her maiden status. Poor boyfriend had fallen in love with Pita when she was very young on the "flower of her age", but as Pita was a very committed family's daughter, and had to work until things improve, so her boyfriend would have to wait for it. But as the man had "needs" and was not willing to wait until that dream happen, he had sought another partner, to later realize that his heart was still owned by Pita. When Pita reached 38 years of age, that old boyfriend already had divorced and returned to recover "his heart" which was with Pita. They prepared the wedding event quickly, but it was not because she was pregnant, but because they had already wasted time and had little playing time, in addition they wanted to see the "fruit of their love." The day Pita was getting ready for her wedding, she look in the mirror in her wedding dress and said "I leave you, dressed in white and with the high forehead, and you shall do the same" (what she implied was that because she waited until marriage virgin, everyone else should do the same)… Ana could not believe what the older cousin had said, to whom she would be referring to? If most of the cousins already "had eaten cake before recess? (Most of them had lost their virginity prior to get married) Well, Ana thought to herself, people have their own way of being happy.

THE PERSISTENCE AS A PATH TO PROGRESS

The following year, Ana had reached her 16 but as it was not "an adult", for employment purposes she was not qualified to earn the "minimum wage." Employers did not pay even the minimum wage to teenagers. Not only that, but sexual harassment was very common, so whenever she was interviewed for work if the interviewer was a man, most of the times would ask if she was "sexually active." Ana's face blushed, because she thought it was noticeable that she never had a boyfriend (her mind was busy with other worries). Once Ana dared to ask why they were always having that type of question in the interviews, the interviewer said it was very easy with "the body she had" that any girl used it "for its purpose" implying that at that age, all girls or most of them were carried by "hormones." When she got tired of looking for work, Ana had to take a job in clothing stores or even on small restaurants, since whenever she asked for work in offices or stores/supermarkets, the same "offer" was not missing, instead of giving her the opportunity she needed to work, she would get invited to the "hotel," although she never accepted their indecent proposals, she thought that maybe she would never get job, because rather than inviting her to have an ice cream or a coffee or give her the job she was looking for, she received those proposals.

When Ana got convinced that "insanity" could not continue, then she decided to enter preparatory school (college). But as she did not have enough savings, she had to work at least part-time. Of course the comments from the family were not missing. They were saying how she was going to college to avoid her destiny since one day she would marry and her dreams of would end in the household chores (like a punishment). Apparently, nobody had noticed that it was precisely what Ana was trying to fleeing from. Instead she wanted to make it to a college degree and aspired to be self-sufficient and without anyone throwing anything at her face. But her parents and siblings only saw things through their own lens: "To shout vociferously comments." Ana continue attending college/ school. But there was no day that her parents or brothers would not remind her about the "silly idea" of continuing in the school since it would be "very difficult" to get a job for being poor and had not "good presentation." Ana never understood her family criticism because outside of home, she always was followed by men who made "indecent proposals" of work but with the condition of "having some fun" first.

Ana's family was still insisting that school would not serve for "anything", but the more they insisted in that idea, the more Ana insisted in continue going to school. On one occasion, Ana arrived from her classes around midnight. This time, she missed the last bus that was going to her neighborhood. So she had to take another bus to the bus station and took another route. For when she arrived home everybody had already eaten, so what was left were the empty pans and dirty dishes that Ana should clean the next day if she had time before going to work and school. Ana was very hungry because everything was already closed by that time and she had only eaten a bag of chips between classes. When Ana asked what was the "plot" about; they all made circle around her and told her that what was she expecting, since she did not contribute much to the expenses and she would rather being thankful for being "tolerated" at home "doing nothing." Ana became enraged and replied to the parents and brothers that if they had found her in a "dump" and picked up for pity, because only that explained their contempt and lack of consideration. Then the older brother "Chino" told her to "shout her mouth up" ask her to end the conversation. He also said that he did not "believe it" that she was studying until that late time… When the MOM also got into the ring and told Ana that better get who could support her because they could not "pay for her food" Ana then replied that it was perhaps hinting that she would follow her steps and ended so poor with lots of kids and bitter. Then the "Chino" launched his curse and told the Lady, "leave it alone mom, she will soon will end up (pregnant) panzona, and will have to swallow her words…"

It was then that Ana was even more enraged, and replied "listen well what I say, because I'm not going to repeat it, what you just wish,–I say it very clear-you are going to get it in return, but on what you most love."

Chino continued the rain of insults… Ana then told him. "Soon you will get married and the first thing you need is one or two daughters, which will be as 'the girl of your dreams' one of them at this precise age like myself age 17, will make you Grandpa." He then refrained his insults for that was not the first time that Ana had guessed what would happen later. Then Ana's father followed him, saying "I said, women are pure waste…" Ana then also replied, "what a pity to think so well of your own blood, you forget that you are also coming from a woman, and it was a woman who gave birth to a lot of little kids…" Then he said "you definitely deserve a beating" Ana replied rebelliously and told him. "If you hit me, make sure that you kill me, because if you let me live, when I grow up a bit more, I will do the same to you." And reiterate "remember you are growing old and I'm going for strong, so when you need something from me then I'll remember this moment." Don Ira was also ashamed and all retreated into sleep. Ana came out to the patio where nobody see her and cried of rage and frustration then went to sleep. A year later, Ana graduated from preparatory college, and already not expecting so much support of the family, she invite an aunt and a cousin to her graduation mass. They spoke with Igna, who accepted to attend her graduation mass only if they will be going all together.

Ana already had reached 18 years of age and of course the "pressure" of the family did not stop, since she had graduated from preparatory college, at home they hoped that she would work to contribute with money for food. Although they remained limited in the usual way. Ana found a stable job and continued saving because she wanted to enter the University. Of course she was giving a little for the expenses, but for the family was not enough. So the discussions continued. The situation worsened when Ana told them the following year she will enroll at the University. There were various reactions of the family, first don Ira with its pessimism said, "You believe you do not deserve a man to supports you, since you need to study to make yourself worthy of his love…" While the mother muttered "Monkey in silk stays a Monkey." And the brothers just laughed at her saying that she "had lost her mind" since the University was only for those who could afford it. Ana had already investigated the cost of the books and the payments "quotas per semester" And she just ignored them. Ana did not give up and enrolled herself at the University.

THE DAYS OF UNIVERSITY

That long awaited day for Ana had become, the beginning of her career at the University. Her family had noticed that Ana was nervous about the compromise she was about to start. The Sunday before she had announced them that the next day she would start her new challenge. And as it was expected the comments were sifting. Starting from her father who was very eloquent, women are like donkey "the more they study, the more rude they become" Ana replied, "precisely for such encouraging feedback, is that I don't want to be 'a trained donkey'," while her brothers made jokes in bad taste, "Let's see if you whistle or sing." While her mother said, "who knows what got in her mind this time." None of them would give a simple comment of moral support. As you will see, "just watch me" Ana answered with certainty that only she was able to. Although in reality it felt as if she was jumping from "diving board" to a pool without knowing to swim.

The first day of classes, nerves made her "a hole" in the stomach. And Ana was even more frighten when each teacher (for each subject) explained the curriculum for the semester. She had to read at least three or four books for every subject apart from the text book. The first idea that came to Ana's mind was. How will she get money for all those books? And worse she felt when she learned the cost of books and to make matters worse, some did not even exist in bookstores or libraries. Some teachers had studied in USA or in Europe to them was not difficult to list the books necessary to cover the requirements for the semester. After investigating the cost of books and how much they would cost if it was possible to get them, Ana could not help thinking that her new adventure was about to succumb, and that her family probably was right about their predictions, University education was only for "the wealthy." It was then that it came up with a brilliant idea: she would go to every public library and also to the Central Library of the University, there should have at least half of the books from the curriculum of each subject. She then began to investigate whether it was possible to make copies of those books to have them at least in copy. Henceforth it would need to do the same with the other books, buy them copy the most important parts and then return them to buy the rest of needed books. Also did notes and memorized them; when arrived the day of the examination everything came out well. By the time Ana would end the University's career she would have at least four or five cardboard boxes full of notes and copies of books.

Meanwhile at home the complaints continued. It had become a habit to cast into Ana's face every crumb of food she was eating. Apart from the hustle and bustle of every day and lack of consideration of her brothers who arrived almost to midnight since they were "dating" or stayed with friends after work. They arrived after eleven o'clock and on the light and turned on the TV just to spite. In the morning the "Lady of the House," woke up at least at four in the morning to prepare breakfast for her husband and "lunch" of the children if they were "working." The penetrating smell of onion that she used to spice up "lunch," woke up Ana, who had a very light sleep due to other previous years when her brothers woke her with their crying at midnight. Ana would wake up very tired as is she had just going to sleep the night before. Instead of being able to get some nutritious breakfast. She had to put up with all the fuss of her mother about not having enough for the family, Ana would take some tea or coffee with a "pinch" of milk and got ready to go to the University. Which was at about two hours from her home in bus. She had to take a bus that would drop her in the center of the city and it would transfer to other which would drop her on the main road from where she would have to walk at least two kilometers to reach her destination. The situation got worst when it rained and she had to walk under the rain to get to the building where she got to take her classes. She would get to the class socked –sometimes- with her rotten shoes which was very embarrassing for her pride. But no even that would minimize her intentions of continuing her education.

UNKNOWN DISEASE

When Ana was about to finish the first year of the University, her brother was doing the planning of his wedding. Although he did not complaint much of the situation in which the family lived, "Chino" had begun to save because instead of upsetting their parents with complaints, he had been planning "to flight away." But as he believed and saw himself as a "gallant" and as the "gallants" could have any women they want, then he bragged about what he had found "an ideal woman" who knew cooking and making a good homemaker chores. But while getting it, he had left some women with a "present" he had impregnated them. But as a part of his delusion of "greatness" he had another little problem, he believed that some of them would not be so happy about his deception, therefore there would be women who would try to do "something" to prevent his " hit and run" or fly away. And his prediction was that somebody would "act out" the day of his wedding and could appear in the church and make a "scene." With so much stress and nerves, "Chino" became ill a few weeks before the happy wedding. He thought that probably his sins had "haunted him" since he believed in those things. So he check himself with the "healer" who teach him how to do a "cleanse" and was also checked by the medical doctor who gave him medicine for his illness. No one never knew the truth of what kind of "evil illness" the Chino had. After a week or two it eased and he continued with preparations for the happy wedding to be held two months later. Ana observed everything cautiously because she sensed that the consequences of Chino's "illness" were not gone totally and it could have side effects.

About that time, Ana was in the final exams of the first year (second semester) of the University; one morning that she was in her way to her classes, she was attacked by a very strong headache. Ana thought it was the stress of end of semester exams. But soon she realized it was not a common headache, when her skin began to show red and purple spots, that wasn't "normal." So she excused herself to the teacher for that day, and also spoke with Secretaries of the University, so they could tell other teachers why she could not attend the following classes and tests… Ana went back home, she arrived home and went directly to bed; from which she could not arise for the following three or four days. Rather than listening to questions from curiosity of why she was in bed, Ana listened to the comments of her family in the kitchen, "she must be sick, but she deserves it for thinking that she could go to the University and also work, as if it were so easy…" Nobody even noticed that Ana had not eaten anything, and nobody tried to give her a hand when she was trying to rise holding to the walls to not fall, to see if she could go to the bathroom. Neither her mother nor anyone else seemed to care about Ana's status, so listless and prostrated in her bed. Ana thought her "adventure "had come to an end, when it was no longer able to even eat, fever and pain had consumed her all over her body, she felt that pain was spread out from the tip of the hair to the tip of the toe of her foot.

Several days went by and finally her mother had a bit of compassion for Ana and took her to the community hospital (Social Security). But when the doctor saw her immediately realized that it was not a simple flu. Ana needed to be taken to the "University Hospital" since according to them there were more doctors and they could find out what the problem was. The truth was that the hospital was full of doctors but they were all "medical practitioners" aka students of medicine. So they would practice with new patients and illnesses to complete their requirements of the school of medicine, therefore they would not charge for their service but did not guarantee it. Ana did not have a notion of the "time and space" in which she lived. She did not know how they arrived at the hospital. But she realized when the medical staff stocked her some huge needles in each arm with a yellow liquid that burned her veins with the introduction to her blood. With little energy that was left, Ana beg them to stop the experiment, since more than help she felt that it was running out of resistance and she could faint. So the "doctors" decided to conclude their exploration, they said then; "we are sorry, there is not much that we can do on this case, this has no cure."

As there was no money, Ana's mother took her home, in the bus -of course- since there was not money for the taxi. Ana did not realize how much time had passed, but when she got home it was exhausted, and just lay in bed and fell asleep. She did not know how deep sleep (only the pain would make her feel she was alive) she was to the point of semi-conscious, when she lost track of the everyday world. Nobody ask about her health but a friend who sat for a bit in the border of her bed and stayed there and eventually left. No one else asked her if she was OK or if she needed something to help her to feel alive. Thus days went by, until Ana could no longer endure the fever and pain consumed her day by day, also the nausea was so bad that even water could make her throw up. Her body was on the verge of succumbing, seemed as if something had extinguished all the light that always accompanied her. Ana then put her illness on God's hands and told him "I don't know what punishment I'm paying for, and I apologize if I have done something to make me worthy of this punishment, but if you think there is still something for which I serve in this life, please make a decision if you want me to be alive, take this pain away because it is torturing me.., but if that is not your will, let me die now..." After she finished the request, Ana was thinking that her family was right about that "University" was not for her, and that they would then confront her that they were right. That was something that hurt her the most that she could not conclude something she had begun with all the best intentions, and as a result she would break her own promise that she had forged. After confronting all her fears she fell asleep into a profound stage.

During her sleep, Ana felt as her body began to cool, then it felt as if the remainder of her life entered in a single tunnel of deep red color, then her body started losing weight and as if something had fallen off and were floating. The feeling of tranquility had no comparison. It was as if there was no time or space, such as when people observe the infinite. Deep in that dream Ana imagined that "the Almighty" had heard her prayers and that was the end of her life and the release of the earthly problems. Then she was carried away by that feeling of peace and tranquility for an indefinite time. The next day she heard a song of a bird in the window. – No birds were around since there was no room for trees where Ana and her family lived-. Then she saw the bright light of the rising sun. Ana couldn't believe it, she was still alive, and above all the pain and fever had virtually disappeared. Ana had overcome death, she overcame a deadly illness no matter what others believe!

As happy as she was first she gave thanks to God, and then tried to get out of her bed, but as she was so weak she could not reach the threshold of the door, and fainted, she did not know when she fell to the concrete floor, when she got back to conscious her mother asked why she was sitting on the ground. Rather than ask how she was feeling, but Ana could barely answer her mother, so she murmured, "I was just resting." When Ana became a little stronger she went to Social Security's hospital to see if they could prescribe something to recover her strength or energy. The doctor told her that she no longer needed anything and that they had no idea of what had happened since she had no other signs of illness but weakness. The PCP only told her to eat, gelatin and oranges, in order to recover the taste, since apart from the 15 pounds she had lost also had lost the taste for food. She didn't know if something was sweet, salty or acid, everything was gone. Three months later Ana started to recover the taste of food.

As it was very common in the University, students never passed all the exams at the "first opportunity", Ana returned to the University to ask for a favor that they –teachers- allowed her to take the end-of semester exams. With good luck were convinced that what Ana had experienced was a "case of major force." That was how they gave her permission to take the exams as "first opportunity." So Ana was very grateful and passed all tests. Another of her concerns was to keep above average scores, since she always was one of the top students in the class. With great concentration, she managed to pass all the tests except for one that required much reasoning, she then spoke with the teacher and explain that her mind was very weak due to fever she had suffered, the teacher did not doubt that Ana was telling the truth, since he could note it in her cadaverous face. The teacher then assigned her a research project and with it, Ana could complete the semester without any difficulty.

At the beginning of her next school semester, Ana made an assessment and planning of finances for the next school year. But looking at the situation, the shortage of both emotional and financial support of the family, she decided to look for alternatives other than giving up. She then learned that there were scholarships at the University for students with limited resources but with very good grades. Ana went to the building of "Rectory" where they allowed students to apply for grants. She filled an application and presented her scores from the previous school year.

The staff reviewed documents, everything was approved satisfactorily, to Ana that news was like "a glass of fresh water in the desert." What Ana needed was to at least keep her scores up, that was what she had always done. Thus, Ana will keep scores acceptable to retain her scholarship for each semester of the rest of the career at the University.

Among the cries and complaints from the family, Ana concluded the second year of her University studies. As always there were the sarcastic comments of all of her lovely family, "Are you close to flunk? They said, always trying to break the persistence of which Ana had put off long before she became a University's student. Ana replied them "not yet, until you drop" that was what Don Ira always said. Her mother also commented saying "door is wide open, I don't know what are waiting for." Ana then began to think that the constant criticisms of her family might have reach a point, and that it would probably be good to try another solution rather than succumb. She then began to investigate how much would cost to pay a space or a shared room for student so she could be out of that House. Ana found a place in the center of the city. For Ana, it was another challenge, since she had never lived away from home and also out there, would be completely alone in her own without anything more than God's blessings and support. When Ana informed her parents about her plans to leave home, she could not be expecting anything different from what she was accustomed to hear. Her father then said to her, "as good is noticed how smart you are, now you are going to pay rent to another "damn ass." While her mother commented, "good now you will know what it takes to keep up, to see if you can survive," and the brothers said, "Great!, now we no longer have to listen to whom annoy us with speeches of progress." Those were the blessings of Ana's lovely family.

THE NEXT CHALLENGE

**"Freedom as a challenge, only belongs to
whom knows how to earn it" Ana**

Nothing was left in that place which Ana considered once her home; she decided to pack the few belongings she had in her small corner which her family had allowed her to use. She hardly had few things, so everything did fit in a suitcase. She packed the copies of books and notebooks in a cardboard box and told the family that she would return for them later. So the following morning of that summer, Ana undertook her way toward the center of the big city (downtown). She already knew that no one would regret her departure, so just for the heck of it and to be completely convinced of her brothers' solidarity, she asked if one could help her to carry on her suitcase up to the bus stop, so her brother replied, "wow, you cannot even do that..?" Ana was then convinced that there was nothing to hold her back, no one even care about the years that she had tried to be part of the "happy family." So she said nothing more and left.

Ana rented a room shared with a family that posted an ad in the newspaper. But what she didn't know was how "nutty" that family was. The first day that Ana arrived they read their conditions, for Ana that was not a big deal. As she was so tired and all she wanted was to sleep, she thanked them for the opportunity of allowing her to live there. The rest of the day Ana fell asleep, and the next day too. Ana had not slept for the last twenty years more than four or five hours per night, if it was not that her brothers were sick, it was that they went out late and evenings arrived making scandals and noise and did not let her sleep... The owners of the house who rented the room, were "very Catholic" there was no Sunday that they were not at mass. The land lord of the house was believed "high rank" artist because he designed "coats of arms," and the Lady believed she was very "special" because her father's family was well respected in the village where she was coming from. They had two boys and a girl, the children thought they were "very intelligent" like the father. When the family went to mass on Sundays they would make a huge scandal cries and curses were flying like lightning and thunder of a hurricane. In the same way that they were going to mass they returned, recalling the progenitor of their days and grumbling about people who had attended mass and what had happened during the homecoming. Ana thought then that probably someone had made her a "spell" since there was no major difference between her family and the "new family." So a few months later she began to look for another place to live.

Among working part-time and the university studies, Ana managed her time to find another place to live. When she found it, she gave the notice to the family that she had found another place and that would move out by the end of the month. They said that all was well. But a month later after she had moved to another place with some students, Ana received a phone call from the place where she rented the room with the "wacky family." The "artist" asked Ana to see her in a coffee shop because he needed to talk to her. At that moment he confessed that his wife "was jealous", also told Ana to be careful of the girls where Ana lived because they had "very bad reputation," but he could not give a good example of the "bad actions," with the question mark on her face Ana apologized for having a very busy day and departed. Ana again concluded that the "madness" was not exclusive of the poor.

In the new house where Ana rented, there were other four girls. The oldest of all (in the 40s), felt that it was already very difficult to be "fishing for groom" and was satisfied with going out with a man who was "married." The other maiden girl was also thought that "she had missed the train" (she was 38) already. Therefore had two boyfriends to see which offered marriage. But once she had a great idea of dating them the same day; thus she set up for a time, one at 5:00 p.m., and another at 8:00 p.m., in the evening. The one she was supposed to see at 5:00 PM came late and the one she was supposed to see at 8:00 PM arrived early. Both came to the same place, after "they slapped her and beat her up, "for being a cheater" she decided which one she wanted more. It was the easiest way for her to choose the best suitor for her as she later commented to the other roommates. Although the more difficult situation to understand for Ana. The other two girls said that they were "sisters" but did not resembled in nothing. What they did together apart from sleeping in the same room was to go to dances on Saturday night, the next day they looked as if the train had run over them and did not know where the underwear was left. Things that it seemed very rare for Ana, who was criticized for the other girls since she was chased by boys who pursued her all the time, but she ignored them because she had no time for a boyfriend, but they were not ashamed of what they did on Saturday nights... Finally, one of them left pregnant and forced the boyfriend to marry her. Later followed the supposed sister, who also did the same. The one who shared the room with Ana was older and even more eccentric. She used to watch Ana when she arrived from a long day of work and school. She sat in front of her mirror and watched her in the mirror. Ana was coming out tired and would take her shoes off and her clothes and ended in underwear. After that she would rest her feet in the wall since her feet hurt so much for the long day. When the lady would see Ana almost naked, she would start crying. Then she would step out of the room. Ana did not dare to ask what her problem was, but the lady in charge of the rooms told Ana that she was depressed and seen Ana young and in good shape made her sad. One day Ana came back as usual from work, and right in front of her was a big picture from the lady when she was young. Ana acted like she did not see it and continued her routine, while the lady continued weeping. One day, Ana came back from work and the lady was gone. The land lord said that she could not endure Ana's routine of everyday.

Days went by and Ana tried to survive between school and work. Sometimes she was not even able to eat more than 2 meals a day, but she was self-determined to not giving up. The final year of University came, Ana was nervous for three reasons, first because she was about to achieve one of her major goals which was graduating from the University. The next concern was, what would she do when graduated if she couldn't find a good job? And the third compromise, was that she had a "debt" with the family. Although not living with her family, she still had feelings of guilt that probably they had sacrificed for her to share little they had during the time that she had been at home. So she decided to go back to visit them to see how they were. Almost nothing had changed, the cries of poverty and famine continued, Ana realized that with her or without her the misery and deprivation continued. Although they had realized that such horrendous place was not a place to live quietly. Crime had grown, the girls got pregnant at 12 years of age, the teenagers drugged themselves with everything that was put in front of them, the husbands left their wives for someone younger than them, and to make matters worse, Don Ira chatted much with the neighboring prostitute, which was not of much appreciation of his lady wife Inga.

Ana had very kind heart, and forgetting all the humiliations and bad moments that happened in that house, asked her father how it could help a little. Don Ira, her father explained that under the circumstances, he had to look for other "parcel" to build another home. Ana asked how much was needed to buy it, and he told her the amount. That amount represented more than half of the savings that Ana had intended for paying for her graduation and diploma's paperwork. But the desire to help and to reward them the little that they had given her during the time she lived with the family, Ana decided to give her father most of her savings, keeping only the indispensable to survive for a few months. Don Ira did not hesitate to take the money and purchased the new land that was also a popular community, but at least they had the hope that it was not full of crime as the one they lived on. After giving her father her savings, Ana returned to where she lived and went to work harder since she was afraid that she might not have enough savings to conclude her studies, but she got faith that things would be fine since she had done it with all her heart.

THE FINAL TEST

A year later and after many troubles and hardships, Ana completed her undergrad studies. She got a job at the "electoral college" and decided to use the opportunity to complete the thesis' project. With the recommendation of one of her teachers who was President of the "electoral college," Ana got her first job in Government as "electoral validator." So with the help of some friends, she could complete her thesis project and eventually submit the thesis to the judges for her undergraduate degree. With great faith and hope to get approval, Ana had worked on that project during the last year of the University, Ana presented her thesis to the evaluator who accepted it and congratulate her for the good work and approved it. The presentation of the thesis was held before three judges who Ana had previously paid for the simple fact of listening to the presentation. Ana made the necessary arrangements and prepared for the presentation which was supposed to last at least an hour.

The awaited date for the presentation of the thesis arrived. Ana had lost several kilos of weight only by stress and nerves of the presentation. But she had to give her best to complete all the effort and finally graduate. So there was "the moment of truth." Thus, Ana prepared her presentation the best that she could. She planted in her mind the idea that there would be no one that might prevent her from completing her mission and graduating successfully. That afternoon she appeared before the Judges. And she began the presentation. Each of them had a copy of her thesis. And each of them would choose their questions and make them at the end of the presentation. Ana began her speech with the nerves (at the highest) but confidently. Such was her eloquence that instead of letting her speak for an hour as it was agreed, they decided to stop her time in just forty-five minutes. And they began the barrage of questions, to which Ana replied without hesitation. After noticing that she had much security in her presentation was dismissed from her presentation. Outside of the room where the presentation took place, there were other University students, curious to know the verdict. Ana felt like she was about to faint and her hands were sweated… After fifteen minutes of deliberation, one the judges opened the door and I invite her to listen to the verdict. Finally her ears heard what she hoped to hear: "Congratulations licensee have passed your professional test, and become professional and for the same consideration liberated the undergraduate degree of "License of Political Science and Public Administration.""

Those words sounded as instrumental music to her ears. The joy invaded her completely that she felt that her heart would come out of her chest by the strong throbbing. Ana had conquered the first battle toward the road to success by completing her first licensure of her career. At that time it was a custom of the graduate student to invite the judges/ teachers to dinner. Ana withdraw the rest of money from her savings and invite them to dinner. Curiously they volunteered to pay for the expensive dinner. Then one of them volunteered to drive her home. Ana thought that such kindness was not so authentic. But she still accepted the favor. Before reaching her home, the teacher commented that when he had graduated he had celebrated "the whole night" with his friends. Ana try to evade the indirect but very direct hint/ invitation, then it occurred to Ana that her friends already were waiting for her at home to celebrate and didn't want to disappoint them. The teacher insisted no more since he notice that Ana was not as common as the rest of the recently graduated girls. He took her hand and before departing said "I wish you the best in your new journey" and departed.

The graduation ceremony would be held in a "Hacienda" on the outskirts of the city the following week. The recently graduated students had hired a band and a banqueting service which would deliver the food. Each student had paid a fee depending on the amount of guests. Although Ana knew what her family thought of her "achievement" she still bought ten tickets so her family would enjoy the feast. As happy she as she was, she went home and informed the family that she had finally completed her university studies. She also showed them the invitation and tickets for the dinner. Her mother not even saw the invitation, even worse not even congratulate Ana. Nothing could turn off that joy that invaded Ana. So she left the invitation on the table and left.

Knowing her family very well, Ana could not expect more affect than they already–more than once–had expressed to her: their indifference and disgust… And the day of the party arrived, everyone celebrated with their loved ones that special day. The parents and friends of others arrived with gifts and flowers for the graduates. One parent even bought a car to his daughter. Ana watched with a bit of envy as most of her fellow generation classmates had the company of at least one friend. In a moment that no one noticed, Ana withdrew from the Group shed a couple of tears and returned to the group, the good news was that nobody asked any questions of who was with her at that time. So she disguised her sadness very well and conclude the party as if nothing had happened.

Days later, Ana began to look for work in different areas of the Government, thinking that as she had already graduated it wouldn't be difficult to find a job worthy of her education. Unfortunately, that would not be easy, because two requirements that she had not considered were missing. First, she had no "political connections" and as always "levers" were necessary. The second was that she had no experience apart from the "social service." So she requested a recommendation from one of her teachers, who only got her to volunteer in the "delegation of programming and budget" work to practice. For a few months, Ana worked free for them, but then she found out that the only way of getting a job for a female was that she had to be "affectionate" with those who occupied a position in politics, and would also have to wait for many years to be able to scale and achieve a decent and worthwhile place in politics. Those obstacles discouraged Ana a little. But as always her faith did not minimize. She then told a few friends her desire to explore new worlds, one of them had relatives in the United States of North America. That represented another horizon to explore according to Ana, so she looked for a job—which would pay a salary in a department store. She saved some money, packed up just to cover minimal needs, and undertook the "flight northward" to start a new Odyssey.

THE BALANCE OF LIVED EXPERIENCES

All those who tried to destroy my strength of will, my spirit and my soul, as you can see even I'm standing, complete and calm.

The creation of this book took place with the idea of clear many doubts of those who have ever questioned what I was doing with my life. All those who understood it (the book), found stories and anecdotes that people around me thought I would not remember to tell. Starting with my family I communicate them that this book gives them a better idea of how things happen for a reason, and how some events change someone's life. Here you find many memories that shaped my destiny and personality.

TO MY FATHER

I would like to remind my father that although it is true that "life is not a bed of roses" it is not a bed of pure thorns either. God and Mother Nature gave to us human beings certain attributes that no other living beings of the planet Earth have. These attributes include the proper use of the brain or mind, the ability to think, reason and memory. As well as the ability to feel, to express anger, love, and joy to other living beings, and what we call the soul and spirit. All those attributes of the human being well used will help you transform your environment and why not, to convert the thorns on roses, or at least to grow them. This body that by accident or out of curiosity you (father and mother) believe provided me with; was not something you planned but what Mother Nature could create and what God decided that you would be who materialized it. So I liberate myself of any blame including the guilt of being born female, or of not being born with the features that you would have wished I should be born with. If there is still some doubt on it, only take a moment of your time to analyze the situation and circumstances of how I was created and there you will find the answer to your questions. The fact that I was born female does not make me neither less nor more than any human being. While I am not more than everything else, I am thankful to mother nature and the universe that have allowed me as long as God let me exist. Life has set me many challenges from the moment that I came to a light, but it has also put me in touch with resources necessary to deal with them and in most cases overcome them. Every challenge represents a boost to seize the moment that God has allowed me to live and exist.

In terms of the appreciation for what you and my mother called "give me life", I just want to remind you that one is grateful for that what is given in goodwill (good faith), not by accident or as a result of the union of two bodies that not even thought that a baby would come out as a result of their action. Mainly, when what was expected of it was making a "little man", according to the very dreamy phrase "God gives children to whom deserves them", referring to the female giving birth to only sons. Even at this age, I try to remember the good things, to be able to thank you, but for some reason beyond my understanding, I can't remember something that makes me feel that much thankful. Or something that with much authority you repeated, "My whole life would not be enough to thank my parents for what they have done for me." But if I still owe you something "please" I would like to know what the price would be, then I can give it to you so would be like your saying "clear accounts, lasting friendships.

Making a great effort to remember the good deeds. I think in a house of wood with holes that the raw winter, rain and wind penetrated. A ground that we had to sweep to power lay rags and paistle to make a bed, green molding tortilla and beans with weevils that we were eating when the situation was more difficult. Wearing rags and the sandals with nails that made my feet bleed. I think I have to thank the will of survival that God and life granted me to be able to say it and with sadness I say this, I would like to have a list of the good deeds to be able to show it here, but as I never received it so only give a fraction of what I remember.

Regarding the way of disciplining and your phrase "Who does not execute children, is because it does not love them", I've news for you. The use of brute force is used when the words are not enough. And as far as I remember, you never had the courtesy to explain the reason for the punishment. The device (belt) left marks that clipped the skin, which caused such a shame of going to school with the legs marked by the "execution" due to things as simple as asking for a taco, or as going out to take a break of the forced tasks, to be forced to work to deserve even the roof and the food that was given to a girl of few years of life, and who had not asked to come into the world. Father, I hope that your children have given you all the satisfaction you once dreamed, from "bales of money" to the affection of those who no longer exist in this world. And as you said "educate your kids by example", I hope that none of them resolved their problems by beatings and mistreatment. And to provide them a decent roof, a decent shelter, basic footwear, nutrition and balanced education a friendly and realistic communication. Also unconditional love and a guided and reforested and optimistic life expectancy. A road without reproach or culpability of its own disappointments...

TO MY MOTHER:

I am grateful to my mother for the favor of letting me develop in her womb and she did not aborted me before the time of gestation. I also thank you for taking care of me after long hours of waiting for food in the cradle and to not let me die of starvation. Also thank you to change me dirty rags and I healed me when I got sick despite being an infant who "did not deserve your time." Although I believe those favors were paid by doing the same actions by taking care of the majority of my brothers. What did hurt me is that you had never seen me as part of your life, but as a working tool. Nor could I thank the comments of disappointment by having defrauded you and not being born with white skin, with the blue eyes and curly blond hair. I just want to inform you that neither you nor the husband that you chose have that genetics, and therefore I release myself from such responsibility, since I don't feel responsible for choosing who created me by accident or for reasons still unknown... As for the problem of your varicose legs, I detach myself of such responsibility or what happened while I was not even born, I could not control my diet nor my manufacturing process... Digging in my memories, probably I have something to thank you in reference to some prejudices. Thank you that without knowing it or think of it, you sowed fear on me. That fear helped me to prevent errors such as succumb to what others said or did. Therefore my mind focused first on trying to escape of so much ignorance, using the teachings of my early teachers, my mind began to work on how I could change the future. Utilizing education as the first step to escape from such a nightmare, and it was for that reason that I escaped to go to the classroom without having been registered in school. I believe that the teacher knew that, and he did not malice when I arrived with my own bench and I sat in the back of the classroom trying not to interrupt. It didn't matter that I later received a beating at home by having gone to the "street." Mother I don't want you to take it as an insult, but I want to also tell you that life is not only thinking about who is going to accept you as "his wife" or his companion. Nor have to breed all the children that your partner forces you to have. On the contrary, the man must be your compliment to what you already are. He must conquer, love and protect you. From the relationship you have with him, depends the quality of life that you give to your sons and also trace your destiny as a couple and finally as a family. Your children are not born to be criticized or to be raised to then remind them that you gave them their life and as a result they have to pay for the favor. Your children are the result of what you wanted and chose. We all have a choice of life. And you choose your destination and mission in life... And if you still have doubt of why I didn't follow your steps I say it in a few words. First, I never met a man that I would like to wholeheartedly, that was intelligent, educated, hardworking, or think of a promising future and to be self-sufficient, and why not handsome also,(i.e. which do not scare me). Yes, I can see your expression when you are thinking that I didn't gather all the beauty and intelligence that in your mind should be to deserve all that, but even when you think of my absence of it, beauty is in the eyes of those who know how to see (in the eye of the beholder) . I hope that someday you can see something beautiful in your life that will help you to smile and say "it was worth this life." The love and affection of a mother have no monetary price, time or space. It is unconditional and voluntary. The love and acceptance that you give to your children you give it by unconditional instinct and not because you are born to do it, or because they can replace you what someone is not capable of given it to you... Another reason among the most important that I could give, is my own dignity and think there is always a path different from which someone imposes you. Apart from finding and shaping my own way in life, was very important for me to show you that not only of reproducing or making families a person can make her own life. It is much easier to play and do what everyone else does, than to open a path in life. If you don't believe me yet, look around you and think for a moment how many people around you are living the same lifestyle. Now look at them and tell me what are you seen on them, you can perhaps see a pretended smile of happiness and satisfaction? But what I watched ever was "families" who lived in squalor lamenting their fate and destiny, but only that without doing anything to change it. Yet I see many faces that although they smile, very much in the background they had wanted to have other options in life. But they resign themselves to believe that they made the right decision, because only thus can make their life easier. Because it is not easy to accept the things that hurt you, and have the sufficient courage to change them, or at least to accept responsibility for the mistakes of the past, so they pay in the future for it. And that rarely someone escapes to pay the damage that was done to others before leaving this world. I know that I am not a Saint, but I would have never imagined having creatures, so they would suffer what I suffered, neglect, physical and emotional abuse as well as exploitation and the limitation of the dream of an infant. I don't see myself repeating the same story; sleeping in a bed with mattress and blankets, while the children sleep in the ground covered with rags and a cold that reached the bones. I could never sit to eat a plate full of food when I give to my children small crumbs to feed them. And no, it's not cowardice, but awareness of humanity. I prefer a thousand times being judged by the ignorant for not being like them, than to live a life in hardship, and deprived not only of the most essential goods, but the love and acceptance that are the main components of self-esteem.

It would stifle the idea of thinking that one day I would become like them. My dream of living in my house without owed it to no one, always made me fight more against everything I saw. The idea of thinking that I was more than a factory of reproduction or satisfaction, grew inside me as the same need to breathe. I found the answer of many questions in education and why not say it, a better way to live. I could mention many more reasons why I changed the path and destination you had set for me. But for now I can only clarify for the peace of your mind or consciousness to your unfounded fear that if I "like men or not" or that if I am or not "lesbian," I say clearly that although I am not output in a magazine of models, I feel very grateful that the body that nature gave me is well defined and that for your satisfaction is quite feminine and so is my mind. Only you can't never see me running behind the men as expected, because is what I don't consider necessary especially when more than one has run after me.

As you chose your style of life and chose the man with whom you would be happy according to your dreams. I also chose my path based on all that I watched at home and my surroundings. By seen you face full of concern which I never forgot, made me grief of sadness. I have no memory of ever seen you smile even with all the efforts that my brothers and I did to make you smile. I've always had the curiosity to ask if you ever were you happy, and what was what overshadowed your life. See me in your mirror chilled my blood. In addition to thinking that one day I would feel trapped in my own trap, resigned to what someone else could give me , made me felt drown. Your words bleak by saying that a woman cannot survive without a man at your side it burned as fire liquid on my skin. The fear to live in it, was as strong as my fear to live in this world full of misery and ignorance. The doubt of what awaited me there outside made my legs trembling. Your reviews of discouragement and your guesses that I didn't deserve anything in life and possibly even "men" no even liked me since I didn't have the same type of behavior that the girls of my age had, really made me feel the size of an ant. My insecurity was overflowing my skin, which made me more vulnerable in the eyes of those who saw me as a prey for the satisfaction of their feelings of frustration toward life. I believe that God is being my grantor and guard and always protected me from predators and dangers that lurked me always and that would have ruined the remainder of life. After having sought answers in the books and the people who surrounded me, now I can better understand that there is no fault or sin to punish. The forces of destiny are as strong as my desire to make a mark in this life. Something different from what others expected of me. And once again, I reiterate it, life not only consists of reproduced or meet someone, but show a different path and a system of better life that once someone had imposed to me as a destiny.

I hope someday you understand my way of thinking and from the bottom of heart I tell you, nothing more I would have wished that there had been a connection of mother and daughter, but even though I tried during my entire childhood and part of my youth, I could never get it and only God knows why. So I decided to detach from that place that made so many marks, and again started a new path that only God knows where ends, but at least it helps me to feel alive. On my part, I hope that you have found some happiness and satisfaction and that life has compensated you something of all of your investment and sacrifice. You probably thought that I am not anyone to express what I expressed in the previous lines. But I'm not surprised in the least. I know that just like my father, you always thought that I was a very insignificant person, who was not able to open my path in this life, and which could not even tell you what I thought of the system of life that you thought it was correct. I do not remember having ever heard you telling me a word of encouragement that would make me think that I was, or that I am wrong. And I repeat it to you, I am not judging you, you probably didn't know or not wanted to see the value of a human being who is part of you as a human being. Or at least if you did not know the value of at least recognizing it. May God Bless you. Ana

MY BROTHERS

I call on my brothers an apology if ever treat them harshly or unjustly. Hurt me so much having to do so, since I was only transmitting what my parents were sown on me. My intentions were to prevent that you did not repeat the same story of poverty, ignorance and desolation. I understand that you would have to defend yourselves and sometimes unfairly insulted me. Now I also understand the force of the blood and genetics. I hope that those feelings and genetics do not affect your new families. Regarding your support nothing to say. I think those good omens which so vehemently wished me, have borne results:

To (the blonde) person who always made fun of me for not being 'white' with small nose, as well as my "obesity" and lack of finesse, life compensated with other disappointments and failures, that even you have not been able to see them; and as a reward, you married a son of a lady's "gallant life/madam" that didn't know how many men had fathered her children… Your husband who did not know his father and also had Sisters of the "gallant life", could not treat you any differently, and to complete the picture engendered you a daughter exactly like him, chubby (panzoncita) and short and to make matters worse, she was born with the mental complications of the two. There was too much of your expectations (so many jumping) to stay in same place. Well, this is life, it always passes the bill. To the next on line my dear Chino, so much that I can say, remember when I got late home from the preparatory school, it was probably almost the middle of the night, I had taken the latest bus and had no money to buy something for dinner prior to get home. Everyone had eaten and the casseroles were empty there was no more than a package of tortillas in the fridge. When asked why was nor even a "taco" left, you stopped me and jump to the defense of others and said that they didn't know in what kind of "monkey business" I was involved in, and therefore did not deserve not even a taco, to which I answer that if I had been picked up from a dump so you treated me in that way. You, defending the mother said with much authority, "let her talk, when she come out with a belly, she will have to eat her words, and ask for forgiveness for such boldness." To which I replied you, "hope you marry soon and that life will give you daughters so that everything today you wanted for me will come true but in reverse. So your experience it, and you know how I feel now. For what your answered, "now shut up or I punch your face", I said do it if you think that would save you of what you just told me and what awaits you, but the more you insist on punish me, the bigger your punishment will be… I don't have to remind you all what happened later. Twenty years later the life rewarded you with two little women, the first did you exactly what you wanted for me and it was such a coincidence that exactly at 17 years of age, and to make matters worse with the teacher of her class. PostScript the law of Karma exists.

To the poor "guero" who fought to defend its place of male house. And that between your rants and insults called me "gay" and that according to you, it was why I was the culprit of your failures of dating, and also that you were not able to get a college degree, I tell you. I don't have or had nothing to do with your choices of dates, nor that you had not enough character to choose a good mates, or completing a college degree, nor of your disappointments of life. The fact that I had pants well placed, and that your insults and the rest of my brothers discouragements had not broken me or my spirit, makes no more or less than any other women, on the other hand I am proud to think I didn't need anyone's approval or support to form me and be who I am. I feel sorry that you've continued as you started off as a baby when you eat the "popo" when your mother took long to change it. That is life, right?

To the "neutral", I hope that you've decided on something in life, because no one could live always neutral.

To the "grumpy" I am glad that he met a woman who controlled his anger and also give two shoots to entertain you.

The "enlightened one" I hope that so much "light" does not blind you so you can be able to see realistically, and you can see the reality in which you live, so you can provide a realistic education to the little enlighten "iluminaditos".

To the "gentle" I wish you have found purpose in life. And that you remain very righteous you continue helping your parents by taking good care of their home.

To the "moreno" I wish you to continue as happy as you said "as the day in which you were born" it is good that the "bad moments" have been deleted of your memory.

To the "Cherub", I say that I'm glad that you found a hardworking woman who holds together the home.

A LOOK AT THE SUN

I do not like to ask for help, because I know you will decline,

I just want you to respect my survival along the line,

By denying me your love, you tried to destroy my will,

I certainly dare you to try again and you will see.

What does not kill me, make me stronger,

Just try to bring me down and I will raise above to other,

When you challenge my courage with hate,

I am ready to defend my self.

I am a child from the rising sun, but I can be confused by the moon,

When you want to look down at me, beware I already above of you,

Do not try to break my ego, think before you act,

If you try to play with fire, the fire will burn you back.

Ana

"I Wanted To Change The World"

When I was a young man, I wanted to change the world.

I found it was difficult to change the world, so I tried to change my nation.

When I found I couldn't change the nation, I began to focus on my town.

I couldn't change the town and as an older man, I tried to change my family.

Now, as an old man, I realize the only thing I can change is myself, and suddenly I realize that if long ago I had changed myself,

I could have made an impact on my family. My family and I could have made an impact on our town.

Their impact could have changed the nation and I could indeed have changed the world.

Author: Unknown Monk 1100 A.D.

Epilogue:

Dr. Evelyn Marks Psychologist and Family Counselor New York

Gumm's portrayal of Ana's world is both heartbreaking and inspiring. This book provides readers with empathy and understanding. Bookstores with sections dedicated to social issues and women's voices should display it prominently.

June 25 2025

Anonymous Reader Testimony California

The Beginning moved me deeply. It is both a story and a call to awareness. Physical bookstores should place it in their contemporary fiction and women's literature sections to reach an audience that will cherish and learn from it.

June 20 2025

Prof. Yuki Tanaka Comparative Literature Scholar Honolulu Hawaii

Gumm combines storytelling with social consciousness. This book belongs in bookstores that support literature with cultural and societal insights.

June 15 2025

Anonymous Women's Rights Advocate United States

Ana's journey from oppression to recognition mirrors the stories of countless women. Bookstores with inspirational fiction and women's empowerment sections should showcase this title.

June 10 2025

Michael Carter Independent Bookstore Owner Philadelphia Pennsylvania

Books that address societal norms while telling a compelling story are rare. The Beginning deserves shelf placement where readers seek impactful, thought-provoking fiction.

June 5 2025

Dr. Alicia Hernandez Author and Speaker Los Angeles California

Gumm's narrative engages readers with empathy and insight. Bookstores should place it alongside strong contemporary fiction and social justice works to attract discerning readers.

May 28 2025

Anonymous Literary Critic New York

A story of resilience and societal awakening, this book is both educational and moving. It should be featured prominently in physical bookstores' fiction and social commentary displays.

May 21 2025

Olivia Greene Independent Bookstore Owner Chicago Illinois

The Beginning is a title that invites discussion, reflection, and connection. Bookstores that value literature with purpose and impact should include it in their curated selections.

www.ingramcontent.com/pod-product-compliance
Lightning Source LLC
Chambersburg PA
CBHW040831010826
48978CB00012BB/710